Sydney Hodges

When Leaves Were Green

Vol. III

Sydney Hodges

When Leaves Were Green
Vol. III

ISBN/EAN: 9783337052768

Printed in Europe, USA, Canada, Australia, Japan

Cover: Foto ©Andreas Hilbeck / pixelio.de

More available books at **www.hansebooks.com**

WHEN LEAVES WERE GREEN

A NOVEL

BY

SYDNEY HODGES

AUTHOR OF

'GEOFFREY'S WIFE,' 'A NEW GODIVA,' 'AMONG THE GIBJIGS,' ETC.

IN THREE VOLUMES

VOL. III.

LONDON

CHATTO & WINDUS, PICCADILLY

1896

CONTENTS OF VOL. III.

Contents

When Leaves were Green

CHAPTER XLI.

DOMESTIC TROUBLES.

'WHY did you send for me instead of return-ing, Glyn?' asked Laura, as soon as she reached Bruton Street.

Glyn was not one to beat about the bush. He had a painful task to get through, and it was better to get it over.

'I have some very disagreeable business to discuss with you, Laura. You had better get your things off and have some wine or something. It is an hour yet to dinner.'

'Thanks, I had something at Folkestone. I don't care for anything now,' said Laura.

Her heart began to sink. Had he made

any fresh discovery in connection with Blanche? she wondered. There was always this dread hanging over her since that meeting at Zermatt.

Presently she came down to the library where Glyn was waiting for her. He thought it best to plunge *in medias res* at once.

'Laura, I was shocked to find on my return that there were applications sent to me for unpaid bills to a very large amount—a ruinous amount as far as I am concerned. What does it mean?'

Mrs. Beverley turned pale. For a moment she could not speak. She was utterly taken by surprise.

'What a shame,' she said at length, 'to trouble you about it! These tradesmen are dreadful.'

'I suppose a tradesman is as anxious for his money as anyone else.'

'But they had no right to trouble you. I did not intend you to know anything about it.'

'You cannot be so ignorant as not to

know that I am responsible. Naturally, as they got no satisfaction from you, they turn to me.'

'But I intended to pay them off gradually. I am very, very sorry. I had no idea you would be worried about it. You need not be now, if you leave it to me.'

'Unfortunately it is not in my power to leave it to you. The applications have come to me, and I must arrange it somehow. Not one farthing of your money shall be touched until these debts are paid. We must let the house, and live upon what I can make.'

'Oh, Glyn! You do not mean this?'

'I do mean it. I could not exist with this load weighing on me. It would drive me mad. Besides, I have no choice. It is the only way in which I can satisfy the creditors. Have you any idea of the amount?'

'Not much, I admit.'

'Between three and four thousand pounds. You don't suppose I could make even a pretence of work with such an incubus as this on me. As it is, it will take two years to pay it off.'

'You might put by half our income. They would be quite satisfied if we go on dealing with them.'

Glyn uttered an impatient exclamation.

'We take different views of this matter,' he said. 'If I keep a tradesman out of what is really due to him, it is exactly the same as stealing money out of his pocket. Why on earth have you allowed things to get to such a pass? Above all, why did you make me those expensive presents? Owing all this money, it was unprincipled to the last degree.'

'You ought not to reproach me. I did it out of fondness for you,' said Laura petulantly.

'But you cannot be so obtuse as not to see that it is the tradesmen to whom you owe money who have made me these presents, not you.'

'I do not see it in that light at all.'

'Laura, you *will* not. At any rate, what I say must be done. I shall have to see these men, and tell them that I make over all that I can. Then perhaps they will wait.'

'Think of the exposure!'

'The exposure is nothing compared with

the dishonour of the debts. It is the only honest course. I could not live another week in this house. It is marvellous to me that you can.'

'But you really cannot mean to work to maintain us both, and your sister?'

'That is precisely what I do mean. The house must be put in the hands of an agent at once, and we must find some smaller one, or some lodgings.'

'Oh, Glyn, you will never take me into lodgings!'

Laura was beginning to realize what her husband meant. The thought was appalling to her. If he only would not be so quixotic. She began to think, after all, that she had made a great mistake in marrying a man who made such a fuss about a few bills.

'Of course, if you will do all this, I cannot help it,' she said. 'But I think it is very foolish of you, when the matter can be so easily arranged.'

She turned away impatiently, as if about to leave the room. Glyn caught her by the arm.

'Look here, Laura,' he said sternly, 'I don't wish to be more angry with you than I am at present. I have said nothing, nor did I intend to say anything, of the way you have deceived me in pretending that you could relieve me from monetary anxieties, when you have made them ten times worse than they were before. You had no right to mislead me in this way.'

'At any rate, you seemed glad enough to marry me for my money!' rejoined the wife, who was beginning to show the worst side of her character.

Glyn felt a sudden sharp pang at his heart. He had been so straightforward with this woman that her words smote him, although he felt bitterly enough that there was a certain amount of truth in them. This was Nemesis indeed.

'It is no good bandying words,' he said. 'I had hoped that you would agree with me in this business, and join with me heart and soul in the endeavour to mend matters. I now see the folly of such a hope.'

'You can't expect me quietly to give up

the luxuries I have been accustomed to for years.   What right have you to expect it ?'

Glyn sighed deeply.

'It is no use arguing with you, Laura. The thing must be done.   But there is another matter still to go into.   It is not enough for you to get into debt, but you have allowed yourself to be robbed.'

'Robbed ?   In what way ?'

'By your trusted maid Annette.   She has a box full of your property.'

'I don't believe a word of it !'

'I fear you will have to believe it.   I hope we shall not disagree on this point as well ; but I cannot have a thief in my house.'

'Who has dared to accuse her ?' asked Laura, with angry eyes.

'That I must decline telling you—for the present, at least.   She will have to do one of two things : either let you see the contents of her boxes, or submit to an examination of them by a police officer.   You had better persuade her to the former course.'

'I am sure I shall do nothing of the kind !'

'Then, I shall have to take matters into

my own hands, which I should be sorry to do.'

Mrs. Beverley began to whimper. To have her income taken from her was bad enough, but now to have this accusation brought against her favourite maid! It was Ossa on Pelion.

'I think you are frightfully cruel and unkind, Glyn. Think of my coming back to all this, when I thought we were going to be so happy. Oh, it is dreadful!'

She broke into sobs. It was Glyn's first experience of matrimonial sobs. He came over to her and took her hand.

'We shall be happy still, Laura, if you will only join with me in what I know to be right.'

'But I cannot accuse Annette of such a thing. Think what a dreadful injustice it will be to her if she is innocent, as I am sure she is.'

'If she is innocent I will give the name of her accuser, and he will be solely responsible. Besides, if the charge is groundless, she would not hesitate a moment to open her boxes in the face of such an accusation. In justice to her, it ought to be done.'

' Then will you speak to her yourself?'

' If you wish it I will, certainly ; but, as she has been with you so long, it would come much better from you. And, besides, if she is not guilty, there would be so much less fuss.'

' I can't do it, Glyn.'

' Then I must,' said he, with another sigh. ' Oh, if she would but combat the difficulties bravely!' he thought.

But no; except where her inclinations were concerned, she had no energy at all. To carry out a cherished project she would go through fire and water, as we have seen from past events.

Mrs. Beverley had also another reason for objecting to accuse her maid. Annette, if she chose to be disagreeable, could make some unpleasant revelations—to wit, the meeting with D'Eyncourt on board the steamer. Even a chance allusion to this would be awkward. She had sense enough, however, to see that the thing must be done, so she determined that Glyn should do it. She would, nevertheless, defer the evil day as long as possible.

'You don't mean to say anything to-night, do you, Glyn? It will be such an awful commotion, and I am really very tired.'

'I will defer it if you wish, though I always think it best to get over a disagreeable business as quickly as possible.'

Soon after, dinner was announced, and so the matter dropped for the present. It was not a lively meal. It could not well be so after all that had occurred. Laura was contrasting the dull evening with the life and gaiety she had enjoyed in Paris with her friends the Atkinsons. She began to think widowhood was not such a bad estate, after all. She was at least her own mistress. The future loomed darkly enough for her now, and what aggravated the matter was the thought that it was her own fault. She pleaded fatigue, and went early to bed.

As to Glyn, he sat gazing from the window into the dull street, quite unconscious of the lapse of time. He felt his existence more and more isolated. He had hoped at least that in time he would have found something like peace at home, but this new trouble had come upon him like a blight. He dreaded to think of his future. At best it could only be one of passive endurance. He lit his cigar, and, as the sounds of the busy streets near at hand dwindled to the occasional roll of a carriage, he went out on to the balcony and looked up at the quiet stars. Of course his thoughts went back to Lupton. What were they doing there now? Looking, perhaps, over that still expanse of wood and park bathed in the white moonlight. A great yearning came upon him to be there. It was useless to battle with the feeling. It was the dominant passion of his life, against which reason and conscience struggled in vain.

And it so happened that at the self-same quiet hour Blanche was looking from her window at Lupton upon the self-same stars, and wondering why the ways of life were so dark and crooked when they might be made so fair.

CHAPTER XLII.

ANNETTE AT BAY.

IMMEDIATELY after breakfast the next morning Glyn rang the bell, and Briggs appeared.

'Will you tell Annette I want her?' he said.

'Stop a moment, Glyn,' said his wife. 'I would rather not be in the room.'

'I'm afraid I must make it a condition that you are here,' Glyn answered.

His wife seated herself with evident trepidation in her face. In a few minutes Annette entered the room.

'Did you wish to see me, ma'am?' she asked.

'No, Annette; Mr. Beverley sent for you.'

Annette turned to Glyn in surprise.

'I have sent for you on a very disagreeable business,' he said. 'Be good enough to shut the door.'

Annette obeyed, and waited.

'A very serious accusation has been brought against you,' Glyn said. 'I thought it my duty to tell you. You are accused of having stolen many things—clothes, jewellery, and the like—belonging to your mistress. No doubt you will be able to clear yourself; but such an accusation cannot be passed over.'

Annette turned red and pale, and red again. She grasped the back of a chair to steady herself. Glyn looked fixedly at her, and he saw guilt written clearly in her face. Mrs. Beverley resorted to her old convenient practice of keeping her eyes on the ground.

'Who has ever dared to say such a thing?' Annette at length stammered.

'That I need not mention at present,' Glyn answered; 'but as the accusation is a distinct one, I hope you will at once disprove it. It is said these stolen things are in your trunk. You have simply to open it to prove your

innocence.   It is an indignity to an innocent
person, no doubt ; but it cannot pain you
more than it does me to make the accusation.'

'I never heard such a thing in the whole
course of my life—me, that lived with Lady
Caroline Darling for seven years, and had
the best of characters !   I shall do nothing of·
the kind.   I shall leave the house at once.   I
steal things indeed !   Well, I never !'

Annette tossed her pretty chin in the air,
and made a movement towards the door.
Glyn anticipated her.   He put his hand
quietly on the door-handle.

'Annette, you must let me point out the
position in which you are placed.   If you
refuse this request, it will lead to a suspicion
of your guilt.'

'Will it indeed ?   Well, I declare !   Such
an indignity, too !   No ; not if I die for it !
And perhaps, ma'am,' she added, turning to
Mrs. Beverley, 'you will allow me to ask
if you are a party to this charge ?'

Mrs. Beverley was about to speak, but
Glyn stopped her by a gesture.

'This matter is in my hands, Annette,' he

said. 'I can allow no appeal to my wife. I may tell you, however, that she has nothing whatever to do with this accusation. Now, will you reconsider the matter, and open your boxes voluntarily?'

'Certainly not.'

'You must see that I cannot allow a distinct charge of this kind, made in my own house, to pass unchallenged. It would be unfair to you and to my wife. Besides, if it prove untrue, the person making it should be severely punished. You must put us in a position to do this.'

'I shall not.'

'Do you consider the consequences of your refusal? I shall have to compel a search—a most disagreeable thing to do.'

'I should think so. I did think, Mr. Beverley, that you were too much of a gentleman to bring such a thing as this against me — me, that never did you any harm.'

'You forget; I do not bring the charge. I am only too anxious that you should clear yourself. But it is no use continuing this discussion ; I must ask you once more whether you will open your boxes voluntarily ?'

' Never!' exclaimed Annette more emphatically than before.

Whereupon Glyn rang the bell again, and Briggs appeared and was requested to go for a policeman ; upon which Annette screamed and fell into a chair and pretended to be hysterical. And Mrs. Beverley implored her husband not to press the matter, and altogether there was a pretty commotion in the house.

But Glyn was firm. The policeman came, and was put in possession of the facts. A search-warrant was not necessary, he said ; if the gentleman had reason to believe goods were stolen, and charged the maid with stealing, he could insist on the boxes being opened. In fact, if the maid refused, he could have them forced open.

But Annette refused the key, refused to go upstairs, refused everything, and so forced even her mistress into a reluctant belief in her guilt. There was nothing to be done but to go up without her, and Briggs went with them, armed with a screw-driver and hammer. They had hardly reached Annette's room, however, before she was heard coming upstairs like a whirlwind. She rushed into the room, squatted herself down upon the largest trunk, and refused to allow anyone to touch it.

'Now, look here, miss,' said the stolid policeman, 'this sort of game won't do at any price. I think the best thing you can do, sir, is to give her in charge at once.'

'I shall be compelled to do so if she continues to throw obstacles in our way,' said Glyn.

At length Annette saw that further opposition was useless, and then her anger assumed a new phase. A look of vindictiveness came into her face which was not pleasant to behold.

'Yes; I should advise you to open that box. You'd better. You'll find what you don't expect, Mr. Beverley.'

Upon which she rose from the trunk and seated herself in a chair.

'I give you fair warning,' she said; 'if you open that box, you'll regret it to the last day of your life.'

There was a look of sullen meaning in her face, which showed that she at least felt the force of her words.

'I am not to be turned from my purpose by any nonsense of this sort,' said Glyn.

He motioned to Briggs to commence operations. The whole thing was repugnant to him to the last degree, but now that he had begun, he felt bound to carry it through.

Suddenly Annette sprang from her seat. 'Well, then, have it your own way,' she cried, flinging a key upon the floor, 'and you will have the satisfaction of knowing you brought it on yourself.'

She was perfectly livid by this time. She saw that she could not escape, but she resolved to die game.

'Oh, Glyn, need I stay? This is very horrid!' said Mrs. Beverley.

'I am very sorry, but I am afraid you must, Laura. You will have to identify the things.'

He glanced at his wife as he spoke. To his surprise, she was also as pale as a sheet. Annette's words had filled her with a dull foreboding of evil.

'Do not take it so to heart,' Glyn said kindly. 'It is a most disagreeable business, but it will soon be over now.'

By this time the trunk was open, and Briggs was turning out the contents. There was nothing of any importance at first, only ordinary wearing apparel. Presently Mrs. Beverley uttered an exclamation. Briggs had unfolded a piece of tissue paper, and within it lay a small gold bracelet.

'My bracelet, which I thought I had lost at Brighton!' cried Mrs. Beverley.

Then some new gloves were taken out, a fan, a scent-bottle, one or two neckties, and some handsome lace, all of which Mrs. Beverley claimed as her own. The search went on ; more things were found, the accumulated stores of many months of pilfering. Laura's anger was at length fairly aroused.

'Abominable ! After the kindness I've always shown her,' she said.

Annette still sat in dogged silence. The look of vindictiveness deepened. Even Glyn was impressed by it.

At length they came to the bottom of the trunk. There was a small mahogany box still left in it, which box has been brought before our notice on a former occasion.

With the same vindictive look in her face, Annette rose, and, before anyone could prevent her, she seized this box and presented it to Glyn.

'There, sir. Let me recommend that to your notice. There's the box and there's the key. I hope you will enjoy the contents. If you take my advice you'll open that when you are alone.'

'If it's all the same to you, I'll open it now in my wife's presence,' said Glyn, who was disgusted with the audacity of the girl in the face of such overwhelming evidence of her guilt.

'Just as you please, sir, only don't say I didn't warn you. You've brought it on yourself, mind. Ha, ha, ha! That'll teach you to meddle with my affairs again.'

Glyn placed the key in the lock, and raised the lid. His wife was close by his side, looking on with uneasy curiosity.

Two letters lay within, presenting the curious appearance of having been torn into small pieces, and stuck together again.

He had hardly time to recognise the fact, when he heard a strange sound by his side. He looked round. His wife was staring at the letters with livid face and horror-stricken eyes.

The next moment she had clutched the box tightly in both her hands.

'Excuse me, Laura,' Glyn answered, tightening his hold upon it; 'I have carried the business so far, and I must go through with it. Let go the box.'

There was no need for a repetition of the request. Mrs. Beverley had gone down upon the floor in a dead faint.

Annette sat grinning like a demon. A dull pain smote Glyn to the heart. A second glance at the letters which lay within had revealed to him the handwriting of one. Could it be *the* letter—the forged letter?

He carefully closed the box and put it under his arm. Then he gave a pitying glance at his wife.

'Good heavens! if she is guilty after all!' he muttered to himself.

'You had better call someone to attend to your mistress, Briggs,' he said.

He turned, and was about to leave the room, when the policeman touched him on the shoulder.

'Do you give her in charge, sir?' he asked, jerking his thumb in the direction of Annette.

'I had forgotten,' said Glyn, looking dazed and bewildered. 'I suppose I have no choice now?'

'I think not, sir.'

'Then I do.'

Ten minutes later Annette was on her way to the police-station in a cab.

Mrs. Beverley was on her bed with a maid by her side bathing her forehead with eau de Cologne.

Briggs was seated in the servants' hall with a glass of beer by his side, and with the proud consciousness within of having done his duty to his master, his Queen, and his country.

Glyn sat alone at the writing-table in his study with his head between his hands, and the two letters spread out on the table before him.

And an indescribable anguish wrung his heart, for he saw at length by what a web of deceit he had been ensnared.

CHAPTER XLIII.

THE LETTERS.

THE letters so carefully preserved by the unhappy Annette were as follows. The first
was apparently in the handwriting of Blanche
Venables.

> 'Hôtel Europe, Rome,
> ' May, 187—.

' MY DEAREST LAURA,

' After all the heart-struggles I have
gone through, I have at length made up my
mind to accept Captain D'Eyncourt. I
know you will be very much astonished, and
I cannot say I am doing it from inclination
alone; but my dearest father has been, and
still is, so bent upon it, that I can no longer
struggle against my fate. He is quite un-

happy about it—or, rather, was until I consented. I must admit, too, that George is
very much changed. He has been most
devoted since we have been in Italy, and I
think perhaps, after all, I judged him too
harshly.

'As it is to be, I have consented to his
wish that it should be very soon. We go to
Naples for a short time, and then return here,
where we shall probably be married.

'I thought it right to give you the earliest
information of this important event. You
can mention it or not, as you like. Dear
papa seems so happy in the thought that I
shall soon have another protector, as he calls
it, that I cannot but be happy too. I know
I shall have your sincerest wishes for my
future welfare, although this is not now
exactly a love-match. Still, I did love him
very dearly at one time. When do you
intend to settle in life again? I should think,
with your pretty face and ample means, you
might marry anyone you like almost.

'You will not hear from me again until
after the event. Continue to address here,

as there is a little uncertainty about our movements.

'Ever your affectionate friend,
'BLANCHE VENABLES.'

The other was from D'Eyncourt to the widow:

'Hôtel Europe, Rome,
'May, 187—.

'MY DEAR LAURA,

'I have sent the letter. Be very careful how you proceed. My advice to you is to let him see the letter if he wishes it. I have sufficient faith in my powers of imitation to throw him off his guard, and, moreover, foreign paper and execrable pens are, to a certain extent, a disguise in themselves Another safeguard is that he will not have the least suspicion. You may therefore adopt a bold course. You need not actually put it into his hands, but let it lie on the table or something of that sort, and point it out to him, as much as to say, "You may read it."

'I sincerely hope the plan may succeed as

far as you are concerned. I have strong
hopes that it will for me. I believe your
dearly beloved artist is now the only obstacle;
for Blanche sees how much her father is bent
upon her marrying me, and, with the artist
safely disposed of, I feel pretty sure she will
not hold out long. I hope therefore this is
the last time I shall have to bother you about
money. If you can send me fifty by return,
it will be a godsend. Pray try and manage
it, and mind what you are about with the
letter. Above all, don't be nervous. Success
in delicate little matters of this sort depends
on coolness. Thank Heaven, I was never
nervous in my life.

'If all goes as we wish, I don't think there
will ever be the least reference to the letter,
so we are not likely to be troubled about it in
future. They will both be too proud to refer
to the past, even if they meet often, which is
by no means likely. I have made all secure
about other letters. I shall keep them
moving about, and get the letters from the
Post Restante myself, also post them when
practicable. Good-bye, my dear Laura. It

seems odd to look back on the past and think of what we are now arranging. However, all's well that ends well.

'Yours affectionately,

'G.'

'I give you fair warning, sir. If you open that box you'll regret it to the last day of your life.'

Those words of Annette's were ringing in Glyn's ears as he sat gazing with dazed eyes on the letters before him. The maid had indeed left him a legacy which would embitter all his future life. He could hardly bring himself to believe the horrible deceit which had entrapped him, although it was now revealed to him in all its naked hideousness.

The thought that he had sold himself to a woman utterly false and bad, who was guilty of lie upon lie, who was in some mysterious way closely associated with the villain who had ruined his life, was more than he could bear. He sat hour after hour with his hands pressed upon his throbbing temples, utterly

unable to see his way through the labyrinth
of deceit which surrounded him.

'What does it mean?' he cried. 'What
is this horrible wickedness which has en-
tangled me soul and body? What shall I
do? Where turn for one ray of comfort?'

Then indignation, strong and burning, rose
up within him. He would go to his wife at
once. He would wring from her the secret
of this devilish bond which existed between
her and this man. Thoughts too dark to
shape themselves in words darted across
his mind. 'Great Heaven!' he exclaimed,
'have I sold myself to a woman who is the
creature of a man like that! This time she
shall speak the truth, or I will not answer
for the consequences.'

He passed upstairs to his wife's room with
rapid strides. She was in bed by this time,
but a maid still sat by her side, occasionally
handing her restoratives from a small table
close by. Glyn motioned to her to leave the
room.

Abject terror was in the wife's face. She

strove hard to hide it, and moaned feebly, as if in pain.

Glyn had, as we know, a soft heart, but endurance had been taxed to its utmost limits, and his heart was turned to stone now.

'I have read those letters,' he said. 'You married me with a lie upon your lips. I have not come to waste reproaches on you. I mean to know what this bond is between you and that man.'

His voice was deep and hoarse, but there was a tone in it which told his wife that denial was useless. She tried evasion.

'Oh, Glyn, don't let us have a scene. I am feeling wretchedly ill. Give me the eau de Cologne.'

Glyn sat down on the side of the bed and grasped her wrist.

'Laura, if you died in the next hour, I would wring this secret from you. In some way you have allied yourself with this man— this scoundrel—whom I hate even to name! I ask again, what is this mystery?'

There was no response.

'If I sit here all night I *will* know! Your

silence confirms my worst suspicions. Is he your lover?'

She started up.

' No, as Heaven is my witness!' she said.

Her words bore the impress of truth. Glyn knew not what to think.

' Then, what is it? Why does he address you by your Christian name? How dare he ask you for money?'

No answer.

' If I wring the answer from you by force, I will know!' said Glyn, tightening his grip. ' I gave you the chance of peace at Zermatt. You lied to me again. As sure as death you shall not do so now!'

He set his teeth hard. His whole soul was relentless. His very nature seemed changed.

' I did not tell you the truth because I wished to live at peace with you—because I loved you, Glyn.'

' Ah!' cried he. ' You defile the name of love by telling me so—you, whose married life has been a living lie. Once more, will you tell me what this means?'

' I cannot—oh, you hurt me !'

Glyn flung the arm from him and rose. The fierce anger that shook him from head to foot was literally like madness. He was wrought to that pitch which has before now ended in murder, even in generous minds.

He looked wildly around him, and then for one brief instant drooped his face upon his hands and strove hard for calm.

' May God keep me in my senses !' he said.

Then he turned again to his wife. She lay with white face and trembling limbs half turned from him. She was afraid to think what might follow.

She was but a weak, miserable, erring woman, after all, and wretched as far as her nature would let her feel wretchedness. She began to sob.

' Laura,' said Glyn, returning to the bed, ' I will give you one more chance. If you will tell me the truth, the whole truth, now, I will strive with all my might to forgive you in the after-time. If you refuse me, I will never enter your doors again. This is the last time I will ask you. What hold has this man upon you ?'

'I cannot tell you, Glyn. I can only say that I have nothing to be ashamed of, and that I hate the very sight of him, the very sound of his name.'

She broke out into wild sobbings, and pressed her hands upon her face.

Glyn rose up. The passion had died out of his face, leaving it white as marble. Without another word he passed out of the room.

Laura started up in bed, her eyes streaming with tears, her lips quivering with anguish, this time unfeigned.

'Oh, Glyn, Glyn, you will not leave me !'

His footsteps died away on the stairs, and two minutes after she heard him open the hall-door.

Then she sprang from the bed, and in frantic terror ran out to the landing.

' Glyn, for pity's sake come back !'

The words came too late—the only response was the slamming of the hall-door below.   Laura flew to the window and threw it up.

Glyn was pacing rapidly along the street without once looking back.

A scream rose to the wife's lips, but a deadly faintness seized her heart ere it was uttered.   The next moment she lay senseless ' on the floor.

*   *   *   *   *

Late that night a messenger brought the following from her husband :

'I shall keep my word.   I shall never voluntarily see your face again.   I shall arrange with your lawyer to set aside two-thirds of your income for the payment of your debts.   Let me advise you for your own sake not to attempt to interfere with this arrangement.   Let me also advise you to have no further communication with that man.   I have his letter.   If I am not obeyed I shall make it the ground of an action.   It will there-fore depend upon yourself whether you are spared this exposure.

'GLYN.'

Laura's was not a nature to indulge in grief for any lengthened period. The letter found her sitting up in bed sipping warm port wine and water.

After reading the letter she sobbed herself to sleep, thinking herself the most wretched and the most ill-treated woman in the world.

CHAPTER XLIV.

GLYN TAKES HIS DEPARTURE.

Not knowing or thinking where he was going, Glyn pursued his way through Berkeley Square, and so still westward into the Park. Rain began to descend, but he heeded it not. With bent head, and in a dull stupor which saved him from the racking misery of the last few hours, he walked on. He had no definite object in view. He made no effort to concentrate his thoughts in any one direction. His whole life seemed utterly and hopelessly adrift, and for the present, at least, he could not even attempt to shape its future.

The hours dragged slowly by, the rain had settled to a dull drizzle, and a thick fog fell upon the vast district of London and its surroundings. Glyn had wandered on through the rain and mist, making a long round and instinctively going farther and farther from London. The only idea which shaped itself into anything like form was that of not going back.

Towards nightfall he found himself at a roadside tavern close to Ealing. The mental torture he had undergone, his prolonged walk, and the wretched weather told on him at last. He felt he could go no further.

He turned into the bar and asked if he could have accommodation for the night.

The landlord looked at him somewhat suspiciously. The arrival of a stranger on foot in such weather and without any baggage was odd, to say the least of it. Glyn, however, was well and fashionably dressed, and could not be taken for anything but a gentleman. The required accommodation was therefore forthcoming.

' I should like a private room if you have it,' he said. ' I am rather wet, too. You can let me have a fire, I suppose ?'

' Yes, sir.   Jane, get the fire lit in No. 3.
What would you like to take, sir ?'

' Oh, anything you happen to have.   Some
cold meat will do.'

He had become conscious that he was wet
through, but having no change of clothing, he
at first said nothing about it.   He could sit
by the fire until he was dry.   It really
mattered little now.   It is surprising how
insignificant bodily discomforts become in
the presence of a great trouble.

Glyn swallowed some cold meat and a
tankard of ale, and then sat down by the fire.
The horrible depression he had undergone
caused his blood to stagnate in spite of the
exercise of walking, and he shivered even in
front of the fire.   He took off his coat and
waistcoat, and, borrowing a coat of the landlord, sent his own down to be dried.   The boots
provided him with slippers, and although
decidedly moist with respect to his nether
garments, he was not altogether uncomfort-
able as he sat with outstretched legs before
the cheerful blaze.

He seemed to have reached the end of

everything.   He was so utterly alone — so completely shipwrecked on the voyage of life. What was he to do? where go?

Of course he knew he would have to set up his easel again.   He had no other means of support.   But he turned from the thought now with a shudder.   No man can work without some incentive, some hope; but Glyn had neither.   He did not care to work to live, for life was valueless, and the future was without hope.

Naturally his thoughts turned to Lupton, but that was the last place he could go to now.   The marriage tie, his duty to his wife, had been before him in his recent visit, and had acted, to some extent, as a restraining influence on his love for Blanche.   But now this influence was withdrawn.   He had left his wife for ever.   He no longer owed allegiance to one so utterly false and bad. He knew, therefore, he could not trust himself at Lupton.

He had failed to wring from his wife the secret of her connection with D'Eyncourt. Turn where he would, he felt himself defeated. Between them they had managed to wreck his life ; but it at least brought him this consolation, that he was a comparatively free man. He would not now have to endure the incessant torture of an assumption of affection where it did not exist.

Where could he go ? Where recommence his labours ? He thought the best plan would be to go abroad, and take Kate with him, but this idea was no sooner formed than abandoned. If he took Kate away from Lupton, it would be like the severance of the last tie between himself and the woman he loved, and he could not yet make up his mind to this. No ; the best plan would be to go abroad alone.

Then suddenly the thought of Grace Hurst and the proposed exhumation came into his head, and it brought some sense of relief. The events of the day had driven all this from his mind. Now that he had time to think, it all came back again. Here was something to do, at all events—something to divert his wretched thoughts. He would go to Worthing in the morning.

'What was his wife about?' he wondered.
'Would she be foolish enough to think he
would relent and return to her? Would
they be sitting up for him in Bruton Street?'

He had not thought of this before. It
was as well to settle that matter, at any
rate.

He rang for writing materials, and penned
the letter which we have already seen. Then
he summoned the boots.

'There is no post to town to-night, I
suppose.'

'Not for delivery to-night, sir.'

'Ah—I suppose you could find me a
messenger to take a note to town. Is there
a train up shortly?'

'Yes, sir; there's one at eight fifty-six.
I could take up the note, sir, if you wish.'

'Thanks. I should be much obliged if
you can. It is important.'

'I'll go at once. Where is it, sir?'

'Bruton Street.'

'All right, sir. You may depend on
me.'

Glyn took a handful of money from his

pocket, and selected some silver to give to the man.   As he did so, he displayed four or five sovereigns among the silver.

Boots took the note, and read the address.

'Any answer, sir?'

'No; merely leave it.   Do not wait on any account.'

'Very well, sir.'

Boots went direct to the landlord.

'You thought the gent upstairs was down on his luck.   He's got a pocket full of money, any way.   He's sending me up with a note to Bruton Street.   It's my belief he's a swell.'

The information seemed agreeable to mine host.   He immediately went upstairs, and put his whole toilet at Glyn's disposal.

Now, the payment to boots awakened a new idea in Glyn's sensitive mind.   That money which he held in his hand belonged by right to his wife; the ring upon his finger had come from her also.

The thought troubled him.   It was not endurable that he should be beholden to her even to the extent of sixpence.   He carefully counted the coins, and then sat down to think.

Presently he got up, and went again to the table where he had written his letter. He took another sheet of paper, and wrote the following :

'MY DEAR MISS VENABLES,

'I have left my wife for ever. You must know it sooner or later, so I may as well tell you at once. At present I am incapable of explaining why, but I will send all particulars to Kate shortly. I will only say now that circumstances have come to my knowledge which prove her guilty of treachery and deceit of the worst kind. Such, indeed, as I cannot overlook.

'My chief object in writing now is to ask a favour. I cannot touch that woman's money, and I am without any means. Will you lend me twenty pounds until I can see my way a little ?'

'By the way, where is she to send it ?' said Glyn, as he finished the note. 'The best plan will be to post it when I reach Worthing to-morrow. I don't even know the name of a hotel there now.'

He addressed the letter, and put it in his pocket. Then, feeling utterly worn out, he went to bed. He had hardly laid himself down, when he was seized with a violent fit of shivering—so violent, indeed, that he shook the very bed.

'What is the meaning of this?' said Glyn, with his teeth chattering so that he could hardly frame the words.

The meaning of it was, that a man cannot undergo the mental torture Glyn had endured that day, and afterwards walk in the rain for several hours, and wind up by sitting before a fire in wet clothes, without the body resenting the undue strain which is put upon it. He managed, by piling things upon the bed, to get over the shivering, and, being thoroughly exhausted, he also slept; but when he woke in the morning he was hot and feverish, and more fit to go into a doctor's hands than to resume his wanderings.

This was his last thought, however. He swallowed a cup of tea, and paid his reckoning. Then he took an early train to town, and booked himself for Worthing.

His clothes were not thoroughly dry even now. His head was still hot and aching, so of course he sat with the window open and a cold draught of air coming in upon him all the way down the line. When he reached Worthing, he began to realize that he really was feeling seriously ill. He was confused in his ideas, and walked with a weak, uncertain step, and all the while his head was throbbing as if his temples would burst.

He managed to get to a shop, where he purchased a few necessary articles of underclothing and a small bag. Then he made his way to the nearest hotel, and, seeking a private room, threw himself upon a couch. He would rest a bit and get some lunch before calling on Mr. Norwood.

An hour or two after a waiter came down to the landlady.

' Please 'um, would you step upstairs to the

gent in No. 9 ? He's going on uncommon queer ; I think he's off his head.'

Before night Glyn was indeed off his head, and in bed, with a doctor in attendance.

' He is very seriously ill—in a high fever, in fact. His friends should be sent for,' said the doctor.

' We don't know who he is,' said the land-lady.

' He must have some papers or cards about him by which we can identify him, surely,' said the doctor. ' It won't do to stand on ceremony.'

Whereupon Glyn's pockets were searched, and the letter addressed to Blanche Venables found therein.

An hour later a boy ran up from Harley-ford to Lupton with a telegram.

' Landlord of —— Hotel, Worthing, to Miss Venables, Lupton Park, Harleyford.

' Gentleman named Beverley dangerously ill here. Some friend ought to come at once.'

CHAPTER XLV.

A GOOD ANGEL.

IT was one of those glorious days in mid-October which come to our variable clime now and then like the Indian summer. The air was warm and still, the sky more intensely blue even than in the white, hot days of August. There was a glory of gold over the woods of Lupton, such as Glyn had never before seen, and on this particular morning he lay on a couch on the terrace looking far out over those golden woods, while Kate sat by his side working.

They had brought him to Lupton as soon as he was well enough to be moved. He had passed very near to those mysterious gates which, once entered, are never repassed.

The very shadow of them which had fallen upon him had so taken the life out of him that his nearest friends would scarcely have known him. His figure had shrunk to half its former dimensions ; his cheeks were hollow, and his eyes sunk deep into his head. The fever had done its best to put out the lamp of life altogether.

' I suppose it was an awfully near shave, Kate,' he said. ' By Jove ! just look at my fingers. Why, they are hardly bigger than yours. There is scarcely anything of me left.'

' Quite enough to take care of,' said Kate, drawing the rugs around him. ' You know you are only out on condition that you keep yourself well wrapped up.'

Glyn submitted like a child.

' You have been very good to me, Kate,' he said, taking her hand ; ' one ought to be thankful under all circumstances with such a sister.'

' And such a friend, Glyn.'

' Ah ! I can't talk about that ; I should make a goose of myself. Why doesn't she come ?' he added, looking restlessly around.

'She will presently, dear. I have some things to say to you first—things that I could not tell you before her. I have not been allowed to tell you anything before, and now you must not excite yourself too much.'

'Why, what has happened?'

'A great many things, of course, in this long interval. You know you have been ill seven weeks.'

'Is it so much? I suppose it must be. It seems like a dream to me, and I don't want to wake up yet. If it is anything to wake me, I don't much care to hear it. Is it about that woman?'

'Not much about her; she has gone abroad. I believe she intends to stay there.'

'Thank God! But how did you know this?'

'After you had been ill some days, there came a letter from her, which was sent on to me at Worthing. It was to ask if I knew where you were, as the tradesmen to whom she owed money were threatening proceedings because they had received no answer from you.   She said she intended leaving for the Continent.'

'I presume she didn't tell you why I left her.'

'We know that, Glyn.   We found those letters among others in your pocket-book. You were so ill that—that we did not know what might happen.'

'And you think I was justified?'

'I do not see how you could possibly live with her after all that.'

'Does Blanche think so?'

'Yes.'

'Well, about the tradesmen,' said Glyn, after a pause.   'Have they issued writs against me?   They had better attach my person in its present condition.'

He gave a bitter laugh.   The remembrance of those last experiences of London came back to him like a black shadow.

'Hush, Glyn!   I cannot go on if you do not hear me quietly.'

'I am all obedience.   What was done?'

'Blanche went up to town and saw her lawyer on the subject.'

' Blanche did ?'

' Yes.'

' Well, what happened ?   Did she gain time for me ?'

' She paid the money.'

Glyn turned half round on his couch with a strange look.

' Paid the money !' he gasped.   ' Paid over three thousand pounds ?'

' Yes, every farthing of it.'

Glyn was so silent that Kate looked up in surprise.   His lips were quivering, and his eyes moist with tears.

' God bless her for her good deed !' he said at length.   ' But, Kate, this must not be. She must be repaid.   And yet, God help me ! I am powerless to do so now.'

' Stop, Glyn ; I have a more cheerful subject than this to talk about, something that will relieve your mind greatly.'

' What is it ?'

' Blanche found a letter for you at Bruton Street.   She brought it down, and I opened it.   It was from Mr. Norwood.'

' Well ?'

'He said he had obtained the necessary permission for exhuming the body, and wished you to come.'

'Yes; what did you do?' said Glyn, sitting up again.

'Glyn darling, do let me beg you to be still. I dare not go on if you don't.'

'Well, there then,' said Glyn, lying down again. 'Now go on. I am quite obedient —only don't keep me in suspense.'

'Blanche went to Mr. Norwood at once and explained matters. He was very sorry to hear of your illness, but he said it need not delay proceedings, as there was no necessity for you to be actually present.'

'Well?'

'So Blanche gave him instructions to proceed on my authority.'

'And has the body been taken up?' broke in Glyn eagerly.

'Yes—and the will found.'

'Is it possible? In the coffin?'

'In the coffin—under the body.'

'And in favour of my mother—and us?'

'Yes.'

' Oh, thank Heaven ! thank Heaven !'

In spite of his efforts to be calm, Glyn had risen up again and was gazing with eager eyes at his sister.

' And does Mr. Norwood say it is all right ?'

' Well, not quite that, Glyn. There are certain formalities to be gone through. We have to prove our identity.'

' That's easy enough, I should think.'

' Not so easy as you imagine,' said another voice behind him.

Glyn turned at the sound, and a bright smile came upon his face. Blanche had come up quietly across the grass. Glyn put out his hand.

' How awfully good you have been to me ! What can I ever say or do to prove my gratitude ?' he said, his eyes still moist with tears.

' I shall be angry with Kate for having told you, if you say one word more,' Blanche said, as she seated herself. ' Now I have interrupted your conversation at a most critical point. You say it is easy to prove your identity. You must make haste and get well, then, to begin with, for you don't look by any means yourself yet.'

'And there are real difficulties, Glyn,' Kate said. 'It seems we must produce certificates of our darling mother's marriage and of our baptism. Have you any idea where she was married?'

'Not the remotest. But it can be easily ascertained.'

'Not so easily. It seems an odd thing, but Mr. Norwood says very few people do know where their parents were married.'

'But an advertisement would find it.'

'It seems not in this case. Two or three advertisements have already appeared, but there has been no response.'

'I hope to Heaven there is not to be a hitch, after all,' said Glyn.

'We must have patience,' struck in Blanche. 'I have no doubt it will all come right.'

'I hope it may,' said Glyn. 'I have another and stronger motive now for wishing to get the property.'

Blanche read his thoughts.

'Mr. Beverley, if we are to remain good friends, you will make no further reference to that subject,' she said. 'I shall be seriously offended if you do. It has been a great pleasure to me to help you. It has caused me no inconvenience, but it will really pain me if you dwell on it.'

Glyn only replied with another look of gratitude, but not a word did he say.

'Mr. Norwood thinks it probable that the marriage took place in some out-of-the-way place in the country,' said Kate. 'It was a sort of runaway match, I believe. I gathered as much from what dear mamma once said to me. Her brother was very much opposed to it. In fact, they were never very good friends after.'

'We must be able to get information in some way,' said Glyn. 'I must set to work as soon as I am strong enough. There must be people about the Glyns' place who would be able to tell.'

'Mr. Norwood has made every inquiry,' Kate answered.

'At any rate, I shall not give it up.   I shall not be defeated at the last moment.'

' There is a letter from Sib,' said Blanche. 'She wishes to come back, now we are all here again.   Poor girl !   She is not happy at home. She will never be happy anywhere, I fear.'

There was a step upon the gravel behind them, and the next moment Forbes came into view round an angle of the house.

' Mr. Forbes, you have given us a surprise!' said Blanche, as they were all shaking hands. ' Where have you come from ?'

' I'm stopping with my friend D'Arcy at Welmington.   Thought I would ride over and look you up.   I say, Beverley, you're looking awfully seedy, don't you know !   You must have another cruise in the *Mayfly*.'

This was Forbes' specific for all earthly ills, mental and bodily.

' I suppose she is laid up ?' said Glyn.

' No, she is not.   I don't lay her up until all the fine weather is over.   Besides, I am not sure that I shan't take her up the Mediterranean, don't you know.   I heard you had been seedy.'

'You will, of course, stay to luncheon?'
said Blanche.

'Thanks, I don't mind if I do. The ride
has given me an appetite. I feel all the
better for it. I haven't been quite up to the
mark lately.'

It was impossible to resist a laugh. As
usual, Forbes looked the picture of robust
health.

So the morning passed away quite cheerfully, in spite of sickness and recent sorrow.
There was a healthy genial atmosphere about
Forbes which could not fail to influence those
with whom he was brought into contact.
Besides, he came like a breath from the
outer world, and gave them all sorts of
amusing anecdotes of people Blanche had
known, and retailed Reginald Barker's
latest witticisms. It took them out of
themselves and away from their own sad
thoughts.

'You must ride over and see me as soon
as you are strong enough,' said Forbes as he
took his departure. 'I've no doubt Miss
Venables will show you the way. What do

you say, Miss Beverley ? Will you come ? I know D'Arcy will be charmed to see you all. In fact, he told me to say so.'

'It is very kind of him,' said Blanche.

'I'm afraid it will be some time before I can mount a horse, judging from my present condition,' said Glyn.

'Not a bit of it,' rejoined Forbes. 'A fellow with your constitution ought to pull round in a week, don't you know. I shall expect you all, mind. Don't you forget, Miss Beverley.'

'I should enjoy it immensely,' said Kate.

Forbes' gaze lingered on her a moment, and the thought crossed his mind that her face was a very sweet one, in spite of the proximity of Blanche.

'Shall you be staying long at your friend's?' asked Glyn. 'I should like to ride over very much.'

'Well, we shall be knocking the pheasants about for another three weeks or so. You will be well enough long before that, don't you know.'

'I hope so.'

'I'm awfully glad to have seen you all. I shall tell D'Arcy you're coming. By Jove! haven't a single match in my pocket. Don't be horrified at my asking for a light, Miss Venables.'

Blanche and Kate had gone with him to the hall-door. The servant went back for a match. Forbes mounted his horse.

'That will do; thanks,' he said to the groom, slipping a coin into his hand.

The man touched his hat and departed. Forbes leaned down from his saddle.

'I say, Miss Beverley, you know I don't ask out of idle curiosity, but what's the truth about your brother and his wife? They're saying all sorts of things about it in town. I should like to know the real state of the case, to stop any evil tongues, don't you know. Are they separated?'

'Yes,' said Kate. 'It is impossible for him to live with her. She has behaved atrociously. We quite sanction it.'

'Oh, then it *is* her fault! Well, then I won't inquire into particulars. I knew your brother was the right sort. That's why I asked, as I like to be correct, don't you know. Well, good-bye again,' he added as the match which the servant brought was handed to him.

He lit his cigar, and went off at a brisk pace down the drive.

'What a good fellow that is, Kate!' said Blanche. 'One of the most honest and straightforward men I know.'

'Yes,' said Kate; 'he seems very nice. I like him because he appears so fond of Glyn.'

Forbes' invitation was lightly given and lightly received. It was suggested as a pleasant excursion for the invalid. How little any of them foresaw that it would be pregnant with events which would influence all their after-lives!

CHAPTER XLVI.

OLD MR. D'ARCY.

ABOUT a fortnight after, Forbes' cheery voice was again heard just as they were finishing breakfast at Lupton. Glyn was quite strong again now, and was sitting at the breakfast-table with Blanche and his sister.

'Ten miles before breakfast,' said Forbes. 'Don't you think I ought to have a peerage?'

'You are certainly breaking out into an alarming state of activity,' said Blanche.

'The early bird is nothing to me,' said Forbes. 'May I attack this pie?' he added as he turned to the sideboard. 'I'm quite famished.'

'Certainly. Shall I give you tea or coffee?'

'Something cool first, if you love me. It's as hot as the middle of summer, and here we are at the end of October nearly. By Jove! there's nothing like a ride before breakfast to give you an appetite.'

He fell to at the viands with an energy somewhat at variance with his usual lethargic habits. The early ride had certainly roused him to activity.

'But to what are we to attribute this unusual breaking out on your part?' said Blanche, laughing.

There was no mistaking the fact; Forbes positively blushed, though he tried hard to hide it by attacking a game pie.

'Well, the fact is, I wanted to see how the invalid was getting on. And besides, I have a design on you. D'Arcy wants you to come over. I got your letter, Beverley, telling me about the will and all that business, and, oddly enough, D'Arcy's father turns out to be an old friend of your uncle's.'

'How lucky!' said Glyn. 'He might be able to give me the information I want about my mother.'

'That's just what I was thinking. You must come and see him. He's awfully old, and as deaf as a post, but very likely you could get something out of him. Are you strong enough to ride yet?'

'Oh yes! I've been out three or four times.'

'Then, why not all ride over to-day? It's only ten miles. We can take it quite easily, and you can stay to lunch, and ride quietly back afterwards. Or, if you are done up, we can send you back in a trap tucked up in shawls.'

'Much obliged; but I think I can dispense with the trap. I feel as well as ever again.'

'But it won't do to tire yourself too much, Glyn,' said his sister.

'Oh, I shall be all right. We shall have a long rest there, and I am very anxious about this business.'

The upshot of it was that in an hour they were all mounted and on their way. As usual, Glyn and Blanche rode together, and Forbes drew up beside Kate, who was a somewhat timid horsewoman.

It was a strange intercourse, this, between
Blanche and Glyn.   Fate seemed determined
to try them with this perpetual companion-
ship.   It was inevitable that they were constantly together, and yet no word of love ever
passed their lips.   The very restraint, how- .
ever, brought them into still closer communion of thought and feeling.   There was
hardly a wish that was not anticipated on
either side, and the perpetual thought of each
was how to make life brighter for the other.

Glyn knew it could not last.   He knew
that when this happy dream was over he
must go forth into the world again alone, to
fight the battle with his own heart as best he
might.   He strove in vain to see his way
through the maze of circumstances which
surrounded him.   Was he to go on all his
life loving this woman whom he could not
possess ?   He, a widower with a living wife !
It was a terrible thought, but the idea of
ceasing to love her never once crossed his
mind, for he knew it was impossible.   Over
all, too, was the strange remembrance that
she had been given to him by his dead

mother. That scene at her death-bed was
ever present to him. He had never once referred to it in his conversation with Blanche,
but he felt intuitively that it was as vivid a
remembrance in her mind as it was in his.
How could it be otherwise?

'If this business should fall through after
all,' he said, 'I shall have to recommence
work. It will be like beginning all over
again.'

'But you will begin work in any case,'
said Blanche. 'You surely would not be an
idle man?'

'I should certainly not be idle. A man
with the responsibilities of a big estate can
always find profitable occupation. But I can
hardly yet realize the possibility of such a
position.'

'And yet the certificate must be forthcoming. There may be delays, but surely
there are ways of finding it.'

'One would think so. Of course, I shall
leave no stone unturned. We must see
what old Mr. D'Arcy says.'

'You will make Lupton your home until

the affair is settled. I am afraid I cannot part with Kate.'

'You are too good to us. Of course, I should like to stay, but I feel it is imposing so much on your goodness. Besides, I am quite strong now, and ought to be doing something for myself. The longer I delay, the harder it will be to begin. I already owe you so deep a debt of gratitude that I feel I can never repay it.'

'I thought that was a forbidden subject.'

'Forgive me! One cannot altogether shake off the remembrance of it.'

'I won't have any gloomy thoughts this morning. Everything is so bright. Let us go on. They are a long way before us.'

She put her horse into a canter. Glyn trotted by her side, watching her as he had watched her on that bright morning when they had first ridden together down to the coast.

How it all came back to him! The freshness of that morning, with its awakening hopes and ambitions. Was it through any fault of his own that his life was now so changed? Yes. There was the one fatal error—the one false step that had darkened his life for evermore. Oh, if he had only been more patient! if only he had had more faith!

'The old man is quite anxious to have a chat with you,' said Forbes, a few minutes after their arrival. 'D'Arcy is going to show the ladies his hot-houses. His orchids are quite wonderful; but you had better come and have your talk with the old man first. He is not always himself, don't you know.'

Forbes led the way into old Mr. D'Arcy's room. He was nodding in an easy-chair as they entered, and their coming did not rouse him. Forbes went over and spoke close to his ear.

'Here's Glyn Beverley come to see you. Glyn Beverley, Mr. D'Arcy; do you hear?'

The old man looked up.

'Eh! Let me see him,' he said.

Glyn advanced, but he saw that his presence had but little effect.

'Come here—closer. I can't see you,' said the old gentleman querulously.

Glyn obeyed.   Mr. D'Arcy looked at him closely, and then took his hand.

'Ah, yes, I see. Yes, yes. You're a Glyn fast enough.   So like him, so like him!'

'You knew my uncle,' shouted Glyn.

'Yes, yes. He was a wild one in his early days. I always said he would be. Bless your heart, I knew him—when he was a small boy!'

'You knew him when he was a boy?'

'Yes, yes—when he was a boy. I knew what he would grow up.'

'You must have known my mother,' Glyn again shouted.

'Nobody used to ride so straight to hounds, bless your heart, even at ten years old! What a boy he was! What a boy!'

'But Glyn's mother,' shouted Forbes. 'Here—this one.   Did you know his mother?'

'His mother—whose mother?' asked the old man, looking up.

'Glyn's mother.   This Glyn, I mean. What was her name, Beverley?' he added, turning to Glyn.

'Kate,' answered Glyn.

'Did you know Kate Glyn?' said Forbes.

'To be sure—Dick Glyn's sister. Set half the county by the ears. But what's-his-name carried her off.'

'Beverley!' shouted Glyn.

'Beverley, to be sure. How did you know? It was before your time, eh?'

'Confound it!' cried Forbes, getting impatient. 'It was his mother. This is Kate Glyn's son.'

'Kate's son, eh? To be sure. Set half the county by the ears—but what's-his-name was the man. Lucky dog! lucky dog!'

'Do you know where she was married?' bawled Glyn.

'Never married. He wouldn't. She wouldn't let him marry that woman. He never married at all.'

'I mean, where was my mother married?'

'I don't know who your mother was!'

'Oh, this is hopeless imbecility!' said Forbes, getting impatient. 'I'm hoarse with shouting now.'

'Don't be impatient,' rejoined Glyn. 'We

shall get at it presently. My mother was Kate Glyn. She married Beverley. Where were they married ?' he added, turning to the old man.

'What do you want to know for ?' said the octogenarian, looking at him suspiciously. 'I always liked Kate. I wouldn't go against her, even if *he* did. Why do you want to know ?'

'Oh, confound it !' said Forbes ; 'he's forgotten you again. He's no memory at all, don't you know. Look here, sir,' he shouted, taking Glyn by the arm, 'this is Kate Beverley's son—*her son !* He wants to know where his mother was married—where Kate Glyn was married.'

'In a church,' said the old man, with a knowing look. 'I know it, for I was the one that gave her away. Ha, ha, ha ! Beverley was a good fellow, I tell you.'

Glyn's heart beat high.

'But where—where ?' he said, in extreme anxiety.

'Ah, that's my secret ! I promised not to let it out. Ha, ha ! You won't get it out of me.'

'By Jove! this is too much,' said Forbes. 'I wish I could shake it out of the old boy.'

Glyn was persevering. 'But it is very important I should know,' he said in a still louder voice. 'I am her son. I'm sure you will tell me.'

'No, I shan't—I never have told. What do *you* want to know for?'

'By Jove! he's forgotten again,' said Forbes.

'I should be able to get the property— my property—if I knew,' Glyn continued perseveringly. 'I can't get it if I don't know. Now do you understand?'

The old man looked at him again with a sort of suspicion in his eyes, but he did not answer. Glyn was about to speak again, when the eyes suddenly closed and Mr. D'Arcy's head dropped forward on his breast. He was fast asleep.

'How fearfully disappointing!' said Glyn, who had been worked up to an intense state of excitement. 'It is evident that he knows all. We must get it out of him in some way.'

'It is quite useless your trying now. He'd

sleep for an hour if an earthquake happened. He always does when he drops off like this. We must get D'Arcy to tackle him. I expect luncheon's ready. You must want something after all that shouting. It takes it out of a fellow, don't you know.'

'This is a very remarkable discovery, if it is true,' said Glyn. 'Do you think he really did give my mother away, or is it the maundering of age?'

'I should say it was true. He would hardly invent it. He evidently knows all about it, if we could only get it out of him. We'll tackle him again by-and-by. Come along.'

Glyn hastened to tell Kate and Blanche what had occurred The younger D'Arcy was also told, and he entered warmly into the matter, promising to do his utmost with his father.

'He varies very much,' he said; 'he may be all right when he wakes up, or he may be as stupid as an owl. There's no saying.'

It was difficult for them to fix their minds on anything else. They seemed so near to the information they required, and yet it seemed so doubtful whether they would obtain it.

'I'll go to him at once,' said Forbes' friend as soon as luncheon was over. 'What will you do? Go to the drawing-room, or take another turn on the lawn?'

'I should say the lawn and a quiet cigar, if the ladies don't object,' said Forbes.

As the ladies did not object, they went to the lawn, while Fred D'Arcy sought his father. In about ten minutes he returned.

'It is quite useless,' he said. 'I can't get anything out of him. I'll try it another time, or you must run over again.'

Glyn was bitterly disappointed, though he did his best to hide it.

'I shall see your father again before I go, shan't I?' he said.

'Well, of course, there's no objection; but I'm afraid you won't get another word out of him to day.'

Nevertheless, when the time came for departure Glyn went in, taking Kate with him. The younger D'Arcy accompanied them.

The old man looked up as they entered.

'Who's this?' he said suddenly.

'This is Glyn Beverley. You saw him just now, and this is his sister, Kate Beverley,' said Fred D'Arcy.

Kate sat down by the old man's side. He took her hand and looked earnestly into her face.

'Are you Kate Beverley?' he asked wonderingly.

'Yes—the daughter of the Kate Beverley you used to know.'

Kate was not loud enough, so the son came to the rescue.

'The daughter of the Kate Beverley you used to know,' he repeated.

'Ah, yes. Her daughter. Very like, too —very like.' Then his voice sank to almost a whisper. 'I gave her away, you know. Very quiet—very quiet! They didn't want it to be known. Hush! don't say a word. Beverley was a good fellow.'

'But where was it, father?' said Fred D'Arcy. 'Where was the marriage?'

'Ah, that's it—that's it! I promised not to tell, and I won't.'

' But you are keeping this very nice young lady out of her rights, don't you understand ?'

' I can't help that. It's not my fault. I promised not to tell, I say.'

His head dropped again.

' It's no use. I must tackle him when we are alone. I'm awfully sorry, but perhaps he may tell me some other time,' said the son.

They saw it was useless, and turned away sadly disappointed. They were just passing the door, when the sharp sound of the old man's voice suddenly reached their ears.

' At Sutton-Colville Church in 1842. That's where it was !' he cried.

CHAPTER XLVII.

IN SUTTON-COLVILLE CHURCH.

SUTTON-COLVILLE is a village which is by no means disposed to keep pace with the advancement of the age. It is essentially a sleepy village. It is four miles from a railway, and has never, therefore, been fairly aroused by the whistle of an engine or the thunder of a train. The men seem to be perpetually lounging about against walls and railings, the women chatting at the doors of cottages. The very ducks waddle more slowly than the ducks of other villages, and the road which runs through the place seems to have been made for the especial delectation of fowls and pigeons, so seldom are they turned from the thoroughfare by a passing vehicle.

The very church, with its ivy-clad tower, seems half asleep ; indeed, it appears to have been dozing for centuries.   It is hardly any wonder, for it is so shut in by leafy elms that it can take no possible interest in that outer world which it is not permitted to see. Twice on Sundays and once on weekdays it rouses itself sufficiently to send forth a weak summons to the lethargic inhabitants by means of a cracked bell ; but even then the sleepy villagers are not stirred to anything which may be dignified by the name of action. They come lounging up in their 'Sunday best' (for only three or four people trouble themselves to respond on weekdays), and hang about the porch in lazy chat until the cracked voice of the bell ceases.   Then they go in *en masse* and take their places, and nod and doze until they come out again.

It is not much to be wondered at that they are not stirred to religious fervour. The decency and order of later times is unknown to them, for the Vicar is eighty-five years of age, and the curate is great at nothing but tennis and carpet-dances.   As there is not much in the way of society in Sutton-Colville, the curate has to seek afar for his favourite pastimes, and the place knows him not except when the cracked bell utters its querulous remonstrance.

Sutton-Colville is at no great distance from Lupton—at least, it is an easy day's excursion. Glyn determined, wisely enough, to take the bull by the horns, and go to Sutton-Colville himself. He had no sooner proposed it, however, than Blanche and Kate both averred that he must not be trusted out of their sight alone—that they, in fact, must go with him; and it may be easily imagined Glyn offered no great amount of resistance.

The next question was how to get there. Glyn had never heard of the place before, and even Blanche, who had lived in the district all her life, had only a dim recollection of its being somewhere in the neighbourhood of Pulbridge. Even the coachman, who was supposed to know every place within a radius of thirty miles, confessed himself puzzled; but he confirmed Blanche's notion that Pulbridge must be the *point*

d'appui by which they must finally achieve
Sutton-Colville.

By dint of minute inquiries at Pulbridge
Station, they found that a drive of seven miles
would bring them to the desired spot.   There
was a nearer station to the village, it is true,
but it involved tedious delays to get there.
They therefore chartered a trap from the inn,
and put themselves under the guidance and
care of a driver who had once driven a gentleman to the Vicarage.

In about an hour the tower of the little
church loomed in sight.   It was so covered
with ivy that it was difficult at first to dis-
tinguish it from the foliage of the surrounding
trees ; but for the autumn tints of the latter,
it would have been next to impossible.   Here
and there the gray stones peeped out from
between the thick festoons of ivy, and an old
sundial on the southern face showed such a
worn and faded front that the shadows were
hardly discernible on the shrivelled surface.
Time seemed to have grown tired of record-
ing its passage when there was no one to
take heed of it.

Glyn's artist eye, however, lighted up at all
this. He almost forgot the importance of the
errand upon which he had come in the en-
thusiasm which the place called forth.   It
was all so unique—so untouched by the damning hand of restoration. The cottages were
all of the tumble-down order, and the tiles,
once red, were tinted with lichens and mosses,
which presented all the colours of the rain-
bow. The doors and window-shutters were
mostly of that faint mingling of blue and
green—subdued by time and weather-stains
—which is most agreeable to the artistic eye ;
and, in contrast to this, a bit of bright red
cart-wheel stood out in bold relief in front of
the wheelwright's shop.

It was a strange reflection to Glyn and his
sister, that, if old Mr. D'Arcy spoke truly, in
this very spot their father and mother were
made one. There had evidently been some
romance about the marriage. How very,
very little we know of the romance connected
with the early days of even our own parents !
What hopes and fears had probably filled
their hearts as they approached this quaint

old church, as their children were now doing!
What depths of fervent love had ' closed in
one' as they came from its sacred portals!
What were the causes which had led to the
secret marriage? How long did it remain
unknown? What heart-trials, probably, had
they not undergone before they could make
up their minds to such a step? It was all
an unwritten history—an untold romance
locked away in the two hearts now lying
so silent side by side in a churchyard far
away.

The necessary permission to inspect the
registers in the vestry was obtained without
any difficulty, and an old sexton was ' un-
earthed' literally, for he was digging a grave
by easy stages. The book containing the
marriage registers was produced, and as
Glyn stated that he wished to search back
some years, he was left in quiet possession
of it, and was requested to recall the sexton
from the grave when he had found what he
wanted.

' I don't wonder at there being no response
to our advertisements,' said Glyn when they

were left alone. 'The whole place seems to be asleep. It is difficult to realize such a state of things within fifty miles of London in the present day.'

He placed the book on the table, and began turning over the leaves with some eagerness. Marriages were not frequent in Sutton-Colville. A dozen or two a year seemed to be about the extent of the matrimonial engagements. He was soon back at 1842, the year named by Mr. D'Arcy, and among the entries for that year he found the register of his parents' marriage.

It was an immense relief to him. He trusted it would set aside all difficulties with regard to the property, as he knew where to find the baptismal register of himself and his sister.

The present holder of the estates would fight, no doubt, or possibly agree to some compromise. Glyn did not personally care for wealth. If he could get enough to pay Blanche that three thousand five hundred pounds, and provide for Kate, he did not care. Hopes and ambitions were pretty

well at an end, as far as he was concerned.
At least he thought so now.

'We must get a certified copy of this,' said
Glyn. 'I suppose we can rouse the curate
or someone into sufficient activity,' he added.

Blanche was turning over the leaves of the
register.

'How few and far between the marriages
appear to be in this little place!' she said.
'Three or four leaves bring me down to
within ten years of the present time. There
is an entry here——'

She stopped so abruptly that Glyn looked
up from the old oak chest upon which he
was seated.

Blanche was staring at the book before
her with such intense wonderment in her face
that it almost approached fear.

Then her cheek grew deadly pale. Her
lips vainly endeavoured to shape some words,
and her hand shook violently as she
pointed, in a sort of helpless way, to the
page.

'Why do you look like that? What is it?'
cried Glyn, springing to her side.

Kate, who had seen it all, was on the other side in an instant, and the three pairs of eyes were turned upon the page to which Blanche was still pointing.

This was what they saw :

No. 135.

1864.   Marriage solemnized at St. Mary's Church, in the Parish of Sutton-Colville, in the County of Sussex.

When married.	Name and Surname.	Age.	Condition.	Rank or Profession.	Residence.	Father's Name and Surname.	Rank or Profession of Father.
April 15th	George D'Eyncourt	26	Bachelor	Lieut. 6th Dragoon Guards	Dublin	John D'Eyncourt	Gentleman
1864.	Laura Tracey	21	Spinster	..	London	Francis Tracey	Merchant

There are certain supreme moments in life in which one vainly attempts to grasp the varied thoughts which rush in upon the brain in a wild, confused flood.   Glyn saw the signatures, but for a few seconds he seemed ûn-able to comprehend their purport.   Then the name which he knew his wife had borne before her first marriage seemed to strike upon his brain like a distinct blow.

'Her maiden name !' he gasped.

'This is too terrible,' Blanche answered

with white and trembling lips.   ' It cannot—
cannot be true.'

Glyn pointed to D'Eyncourt's name.

' There can be no mistake,' he said.   ' The
very regiment is the same.   This, then, is
the solution of the mystery — the horrible
mystery.'

The three stood gazing at each other
spell-bound, neither knowing what to say
or do.

Kate was the first to speak coherently.

' Glyn, you must take instant steps,' she
said.   ' You must secure a copy of this, too.
What a fearful woman she must be!   It is
too dreadful!'

The words roused Glyn.

' I cannot comprehend it even now,' he
said.   ' This is before her marriage with Mr.
Byng.   She never could have committed this
double crime.   I must see her at once.   For
Heaven's sake do not breathe a word of this.
She would be placed in a criminal dock.'

The thought was horrible to him, as it was
to all of them.   They sat with white faces
vainly striving to see their way through the

maze of wickedness so suddenly presented to their view.

As to Glyn, he seemed so terribly mixed up with this tale of deceit and crime, that even the thought of his freedom, which had for one brief moment flashed upon him, brought no consolation.

He could have sacrificed all—even his love for Blanche—if at that moment he could have washed Laura's soul clean from the guilt in which it was steeped.

CHAPTER XLVIII.

LAURA'S LAST CHANCE.

'Worthing, October, 187—.

' MY DEAR SIR,

'I have just seen the announcement of Mr. Dalrymple's death in the *Times*. I presume his nephew, Captain D'Eyncourt, comes into the property. This would be a good time to suggest a compromise. Can you make it convenient to call here at an early date?

'Yours very faithfully,

'LEONARD NORWOOD.'

This letter awaited Glyn on his return to Lupton. He sat down at once and wrote the following answer:

'Lupton, October, 187—.

'MY DEAR SIR,

'I do not apprehend much difficulty in bringing Captain D'Eyncourt to any terms we like to propose. A very painful discovery has been made which gives me complete power over him. I will call on you to-morrow without fail.

'Yours very truly,

'GLYN BEVERLEY.

'I have the certificate of my mother's marriage.'

The next day Glyn departed for Worthing, and sought Mr. Norwood at his office.

'Your letter has surprised me not a little,' said the lawyer. 'I cannot imagine what has occurred to make you so confident. By the way, I hope you are quite strong again.'

'Quite, thank you. I am likely to keep you some time. Are you very busy this morning?'

'I have kept myself disengaged purposely. Take this easy-chair. Shall I offer you a glass of wine?'

'Nothing, thanks. We will proceed to business at once, if you don't mind.'

It cost Glyn some heart-pangs to lay bare the story of treachery and deceit which had been practised on him, but he was like a man groping in the dark, and he felt bound to seek counsel and support. He gave a brief sketch of his married life, and of his wife's previous career. Then he detailed minutely the events of the day before.

'Lawyers are supposed to be surprised at nothing,' said Mr. Norwood, taking out his handkerchief and wiping his forehead. 'This is a very serious business. I confess I am surprised. You have indeed a hold on them. It is imprisonment if you choose to prosecute; and I do not see what other course is open to you.'

'I cannot proceed to that extremity,' said Glyn. 'This is the point I wish to consult you about. Is there no way by which I can release myself without bringing such a fearful sentence upon her?'

The lawyer thought a moment.

'The only way I see is to get her out of

the country—to America, or somewhere. Then make an application to get the marriage annulled on the facts you have just stated. I ought not to advise you to do this. She deserves punishment if ever a woman did ; but I can understand your feelings.'

'And what about him ?'

'I should certainly not trouble myself about that, were I you. I should simply let the law take its course. What on earth could have been their motive ? It is like lunacy.'

'He may have treated her brutally—probably did. I believe him capable of any villainy.'

'But to put their necks into a halter in this way ! It is a most extraordinary case. Do you know where to find her ?'

'No ; but she has probably been receiving her income through the usual channel, and her lawyer would tell me.'

'You will see her first ?'

'Yes ; that is my intention.'

'At any rate, it solves all difficulty about

the property. With this affair brought home to him, it would be next to impossible for him to hold it. You would simply have to put in your claim.'

'But should I escape all penalties myself? There is the dreadful thought that I too am guilty. There is sometimes a punishment for unconscious law-breaking, is there not?'

'"Ignorantia legis neminem excusat,"' murmured the lawyer. 'It would not apply in this case. You have been simply made a dupe. You need have no fear for yourself. A statement of the facts, and the former marriage certificate, would get you a decree nullifying your own marriage without any difficulty.'

With a somewhat lightened heart Glyn proceeded to town. His intention was to find out Laura's address and go to her at once. He was under the impression she was still abroad, and he was prepared to follow her wherever she might be. He therefore went direct to the lawyer who had the arrangement of her affairs.

To his surprise, he learned that his wife was back in Bruton Street. She had returned some days before.

Glyn jumped into a hansom and drove direct to the house. In spite of the justice of his cause, he was nervous and agitated to a painful extent at the thought of the part he had to perform. Through all the indignation and horror he naturally felt at his wife's conduct, he could not put away the fact that for the time at least she had been an affectionate wife, and that she possessed many excellent qualities. If he could have done so with any show of justice to himself, he would even now have rescued her from the dreadful consequences of her guilt. Indeed, the chief object of his visit was, as we have seen, to avert the punishment she so richly deserved.

Briggs, who was still in charge of the house, opened the door to him.

'Mr. Beverley!' he exclaimed. 'Goodness me, sir, how ill you are looking!'

'Is your mistress at home?' asked Glyn, without heeding the exclamation.

'Yes, sir; came back the day before yesterday.'

'Where is she?'

'In the drawing-room, I believe, sir.'

Briggs watched his master's form as he passed up the stairs in some trepidation. He of course knew that serious consequences had resulted from that unfortunate exposure of Annette's dishonesty, although he did not know the particulars. He had once or twice thought it would have been better to have shut his eyes to the maid's delinquencies. However, it was too late now, and Briggs had the consolation, after all, of knowing that he had done his duty.

Laura was at the writing-table, with her back towards the door, as Glyn entered the room. She turned with an impatient exclamation as the opening of the door aroused her. When she saw who it was, a little cry escaped her, and the pen dropped from her hand.

'Oh, Glyn! is that you?'

She was up in a moment, and advancing towards him with her hand out. A sudden hope shot through her mind that this return meant forgiveness, and that the heavy cloud which had been on her mind for the last two months or more was now lifted.

Poor soul! She little knew how far heavier was the doom now hanging over her. How the consequences of her sin had found her out!

Truly, the most pitiable object on earth is a fair woman with a soul steeped in guilt.

Something in Glyn's face made her stop as she approached him. He pointed to a chair.

'Sit down, Laura,' he said. 'I cannot take your hand. There can be nothing in common between us again.'

Laura sank into the nearest chair.

'I had hoped you were come to say you forgive me!' she exclaimed sadly.

'I might have done so in time, as far as those letters are concerned. I cannot do so now. Your conduct has been too vile!'

Laura moved a little impatiently.

'What is it now?' she said. 'If you have only come to renew your reproaches, I cannot think it was worth your while. I know it was very mean and wicked to have done what I did. I have been very sorry about those letters, but it can do no good to go on reproaching me all my life.'

'I am not here to renew my reproaches about those letters. Is there nothing else, Laura ; no greater sin that you have to answer for ?'

'I am not aware that there is,' she said, dropping her eyes.

Glyn's patience was at an end.

'Good God!' he cried. 'Will you go on lying to me all your life? Have you any recollection of April 15, 1864 ?'

A deadly pallor suddenly struck Laura's face. She half raised her hand in a deprecating kind of way. Then she dropped it again, and sat with her eyes still down.

'What do you mean, Glyn ?' she said faintly.

'I mean that on the day I name you married George D'Eyncourt! That you have since then twice committed bigamy!'

With wild terror in her face, Laura sprang

from her chair and threw herself at Glyn's feet, clasping his knees, and looking up to him in abject entreaty.

'Oh hush, Glyn! for heaven's sake do not betray me!'

She looked wildly around, as if for some means of escape from the terror which was over her.   Then she clasped him still more closely.

'Glyn, Glyn!   You will not—oh, you cannot betray me!   Have pity on me! have pity on me!'

Again she looked up in grievous entreaty, clasping her arms still more closely round his knees.   It was a sad spectacle—this woman's utter terror and despair.   Glyn's heart sickened as he looked on it.

'Get up, Laura,' he said.   'I am not here to betray you.   I am here to save you as far as I can.   Though, God knows, the consequences of your sin must be terrible!'

But the wretched woman did not move. Her face dropped upon her hands, and sobs shook her whole frame.

There was a feeling in Glyn's mind which

made him shrink instinctively from touching her—her deceit had been so vile.

'Get up, Laura,' he said. 'I tell you I am here to do what I can to save you.'

Still she did not move. She seemed to have lost the power of volition through the violence of her sobs. Then suddenly she sank on the floor at his feet, her face buried in her hands.

She was prostrate at last—her deceit stripped of its mask, her sin laid bare.

It was a horrible sight. Glyn could bear it no longer. He stooped and lifted her from the ground, and placed her on a couch. She lay there with her face still hidden.

There was a silence of several minutes, broken only by her sobs. At last she grew quieter. Then Glyn said calmly:

'Laura, why did you do this dreadful thing? Why did you seek to blight my life with this fearful deceit on your mind?'

'Oh, do not ask me!' she moaned. 'I cannot tell you now. I was not all to blame. You do not know how I was tempted. Oh, was ever anyone so utterly wretched as I am?'

Her sobs broke out afresh. She lay with her face hidden in the cushions. She did not like to meet Glyn's gaze.

'Come, Laura; there must be an end of this,' Glyn said. 'I have many things to say to you. I do not wish to reproach you. Heaven knows, your punishment will be hard enough!'

She turned quickly, and clutched his arm as he sat by her side.

'But you said you would not betray me. Oh, Glyn, you cannot, you will not!'

'Be silent!' he answered sternly. 'You cannot suppose that you can escape entirely from the consequences of a crime like this. I want to arrange with you how best to lighten the punishment that must follow.'

'But you will not let it be known. Oh, you will not expose me to this disgrace!'

Again the look of terror came into her eyes. She strove to throw her arms about him, but he put her aside, and answered her still more sternly.

'Look here, Laura, there must be an end of this. There can be no further pretence of affection on my part—there should be none on yours. You forget that you are that man's wife.'

She hid her face in her hands again.

' Oh, if I could forget it—if I could forget it !' she cried, her tears streaming out afresh. ' The villain ! He has ruined my life !' she cried, with a sort of wail.

' I can well believe it,' Glyn said. ' Still, you need not have given yourself to him body and soul. But I cannot go into that ; God only knows what your motive was. I shall not seek to inquire. What I want to do now is to make arrangements for the future.'

' I will go abroad again,' Laura suddenly said. ' I will not come in your way, Glyn. I solemnly promise you I will not. Only do not expose me. Oh, you cannot, you cannot ! Nothing need be said. Only let me go. You can take the money—all of it—only let me get away. I will never trouble you again.'

She was sitting up now, her eyes all red with weeping, her hair hanging in disorder about her shoulders.   She looked round as if she wished to depart at once, for a terrible fear still possessed her heart.

'Sit still, Laura,' said Glyn.   'We are only wasting time.   It is sheer nonsense to talk as you are doing.   I have been patient long enough, and there is another to be punished beside yourself.'

'But in punishing me you cannot punish him.   He has not committed a crime.'

She sank back again with a shudder as the words passed her lips.   Perhaps she had never before fully realized what she had done.   That last ugly word brought it home to her.

'No; but he has connived at one, and so put himself within reach of the law—at least, I fervently hope so.'

'But in punishing him you will punish me,' Laura cried.   'Oh, what shall I do?   What shall I do?'

She wrung her hands and threw herself back on the couch once more.   Glyn grew sterner.

'I tell you that you cannot expect to

escape entirely from the consequences of
your guilt. You must make up your mind
to some punishment.'

'But why need you say anything? It
cannot do you any good; and I have
promised to keep out of your way,' she
answered.

'Laura, this is insanity. You must see
that such a course is impossible. I should
be conniving at a crime myself. I should
render myself liable to a prosecution for con-
cealing the fact.'

'It need never be known.'

'Never be known, when there is the damning fact recorded in the register at Sutton-
Colville? Besides, I have no intention of
sacrificing my whole future life to your deceit
and treachery, of becoming a laughing-stock
to that villain D'Eyncourt.'

Laura took refuge in tears once more.

'Oh, what will become of me? what will
become of me?' she sobbed.

'Listen to me,' said Glyn. 'There is but
one course open to you. You must get away
--quite away. You must be out of the reach

of the law when the law takes its course.
This is your only chance.'

'But where can I go?'

'To America.'

'Oh, Glyn, I cannot!' she cried, starting
up. 'Banished to America! It is too
dreadful!'

'There is no other course open to you. It
is, in fact, your only chance of safety.'

'Glyn, Glyn, you cannot send me away
like this! I could not live. It is too
dreadful!'

She clung to his arm again, and looked
into his face with renewed entreaty.

'Oh, Glyn, dearest Glyn, you cannot do
this dreadful thing!' she cried.

Her whole frame was quivering. The
terror of the future that was before her
almost took away her senses. In spite of
himself, Glyn's heart was moved, but he
steeled himself against her entreaties. There
was but one course open to him, he knew.

'We are only wasting time, Laura. If
you do not consent to this, you must take
the consequences. I have suggested it to

save you from the punishment you deserve. I do this even at my own risk. If it were known, I should hardly escape punishment myself. You can take the money; I shall not touch one penny of it. Once across the Atlantic, you can go where you like—do what you like. I do not doubt you would soon get reconciled to your new home. You have a facility for attaching yourself to new faces. If you will consent to go at once, I will arrange everything for your departure.'

Laura saw that the game was up. Her natural pluck returned to her. She sat up once more.

'If it must be so, let it be quickly, then,' she said. 'It is a horrible fate!'

'It was a horrible crime. You forget what it might have entailed. You may thank God for the rest of your days that you have escaped imprisonment.'

Laura shuddered. She had never fully realized this before. She began to feel a feverish anxiety to get away.

'When do you wish me to go, Glyn?' she said with comparative calmness.

'As soon as I can arrange for your passage. This week, if possible.'

'Very well.'

'I will see to all your business matters, and give you time to settle in your new home. You will have to change your name if you wish to avoid being known when the affair is made public.'

'And I shall never, never see you again, Glyn ?'

'Never, Laura.   You yourself must see that it is impossible.   There is—there can be no tie between us.'

Once more she threw herself at his feet.

'Oh, Glyn, whatever my fault—my crime, I have loved you dearly.   I would have been a true wife to you always—always.'

She looked up into his face imploringly, her eyes once more streaming with tears.

'Laura, this is madness.   You know it. Even your words are a sin now.   You are the wife of another man.'

'Oh, no, no !' she cried passionately, 'not of him.   I hate him—I *hate* him !   I cannot go to him, never—never !'

'You need not; but that does not render it the less impossible for you to remain with me.   Even if I could pardon you, you know this could not be.'

'Oh yes, it could be.   We could go away from here—away from everything.   You should never regret it, Glyn.   I would be so true to you.   Oh, if you only loved me!—if you only loved me!'

There was a sort of despairing wail in her voice which moved Glyn in spite of himself. Through all her deceit and treachery there was this one redeeming point in her nature— that she could entertain a deep, sincere love for an honest man.   Poor soul!   She had never had the chance before.   Possibly, the untold history of her life might evoke pity, even now.

'Laura, this is indescribably painful to me,' Glyn said.   'You know I cannot listen to you.   My life would be an acted lie, wherever I might be.   The course I have proposed is the only one open to you.   Let us end this. I cannot bear it.'

A sudden change came over Laura's face.

'I know what it is, Glyn. I have striven to think otherwise, but it is *she* who has come between you and me. But for her you would have been content to make me happy.'

Glyn's patience was gone at last.

'How dare you utter such a lie as that!' he cried. 'If you drag her pure name into this miserable tale of wickedness and crime, I will denounce you to the whole world at once. You know you have ruined her life and mine. Wretched woman! it is you who came between her and me. You cannot— dare not deny it!'

'But you will marry her when you have got rid of me,' said Laura doggedly.

'It is your own base nature which makes you think so,' cried Glyn in fierce anger. 'Through you she is now further from me than ever. How could I dream of linking my degraded name with one so pure as she is? It is an insult even to name her now. You have sunk so low that you cannot see it is the outraged laws alone which compel me to act.'

'At least, do not part with me with harsh words on your lips,' she said.

'I have told you I would not. I have offered to do all in my power. Take care that you do not try me too far. I will give you a day to prepare your plans. Be ready to leave this house the day after to-morrow. I can have no further words on this subject.'

He strode towards the door, still white with anger. Laura saw that all was over—at least, for the present; but there were still three days, she thought, during which he might possibly relent.

She reckoned without her host.

The third day after she was speeding over the blue waters of St. George's Channel in a Cunard steamer bound for New York.

Laura's was a buoyant nature. She was not looking back with vain regrets to the fast-receding shores she had left behind. Her face, erewhile wet with tears, was turned towards that distant land where, under the name of Mrs. Courtenay, she was to seek a new home and a new life.

An angel of darkness could not prostrate a

nature like Laura's for more than twenty-four hours at a stretch.

A few weeks after there came a letter from Laura informing Glyn of her safe arrival in America. Although not in accordance with the sequence of events, I give an extract from it here, in order that it may not interfere with the narration of more startling incidents which occurred at the time of its arrival. Whilst offering no real excuse for her conduct, it may to some extent palliate her sins up to a certain point. Lenient people may perhaps consider that at the outset, at least, she was more to be pitied than blamed.

'You asked me,' she wrote, 'what possible motive I could have in so deceiving you. I found it impossible to answer at the time, but I shall say a few words now in the hope that you may be disposed to judge me less harshly when you have heard what I have to say. You must remember that when I first met George D'Eyncourt I was young and very inexperienced. I had seen nothing of the world. I had not much stability of character, and I was warm-hearted and impulsive. You may imagine how very easily I fell a victim to his fascinations. Few girls of my age could have resisted the combined attractions of his accomplishments and his appearance—for he was one of the handsomest men I ever met. The possession of these attractions has proved fatal to him, for he was utterly without principle. I was so infatuated with him that he had no difficulty in persuading me to go through the ceremony of marriage with him privately in that quiet little country church. It is a bitter remembrance now, but I was in a heaven of happiness then, for I thought he loved me truly, and I was told, and fondly believed, that our marriage was not long to remain secret. Fickleness is the very essence of his nature. I could see that within a few weeks even he began to get tired of me. I was staying with an old aunt at the time. She lived alone in a very quiet way, and there was no difficulty about our meeting constantly. One excuse after another was made for not revealing the marriage. Over and over again I urged him to make it known, but without success. My father died shortly after, and under pretence of paying a long visit to some friends, I went abroad with George. Then I began to see him as he really was—the most unprincipled, selfish, overbearing man it was ever my lot to encounter. He thought I should come into some money at my father's death, although I had never led him to suppose so. The sum I really inherited was so small that it filled him with disgust. He vented his disappointment by subjecting me to the vilest course of treatment it is possible to conceive. I can never describe my wretchedness. It was almost more than I could endure. I no longer regretted that my marriage had been secret, for I felt that life with him would be simply unendurable, and I resolved to leave him whenever I could find the chance. We returned to England and went into lodgings. I found that George was deeply in debt. This only increased the brutality of his conduct to me. On one occasion, when he was driven to an extremity with regard to money matters, and I felt that I could really no longer endure his brutality, he came to me with a proposition.

' There was an old Mr. Byng, a friend of my father, who had recently lost his wife, and who was sadly in want of someone to look after him in his declining days, for he was an almost constant invalid. He had always shown a great liking for me, and he was very rich and good-natured. George proposed that we should separate, and, as our marriage was not known, that I should lay siege to the old man's heart, and marry him for the sake of his money. I indignantly refused, upon which my husband commenced a course of treatment which was simply un-endurable.

' At length, driven almost distracted, I yielded a reluctant consent. Having once given way, circumstances seemed to combine to facilitate the project. I presented myself at Mr. Byng's house on the pretence that I wished to consult him on some matters of business. He received me most cordially— was so kind, indeed, that I soon began to think that life with an amiable old man would be far preferable to the misery I had endured with a young one. I have omitted to mention that my husband's monetary difficulties had obliged him to leave the army, so that there literally seemed no alternative but to live with the old man or be thrown on the world.

'When once I had made up my mind, all things went smoothly. I had no need to try and win Mr. Byng, for within a few weeks of renewing my acquaintance with him, he wrote and proposed to me. I hailed it as a means of escape from my misery, and I was right. Had it not been for the constant remembrance of my crime, I should have led a very happy life, for Mr. Byng was kindness itself. It is strange, though, how soon one becomes callous to the thought even of a crime like mine. The remembrance of my marriage in the little country church even at that time became a kind of unreal dream, and I endeavoured to put it from me more and more—strove, in fact, to forget it altogether. I was supplied most liberally with money, so that I was able to purchase entire freedom from even the sight of the man who had caused me so much misery, and whom I now hated with a most intense hatred.

'At length Mr. Byng died, and I was left in undisputed possession of a considerable income.   The thought of returning to George never crossed my mind ; indeed, at that time I knew he was endeavouring to win the affections of poor Blanche Venables.   I was determined, however, that she should not be made a victim, and I wrote her an anony- mous letter, urging her to put certain questions to George before she consented to marry him.   With her usual straightforwardness, she showed him the letter.   His manner was so confused that her suspicions were excited, and as he failed to satisfy her that his mode of life had been one which she could approve of, the engagement was broken off.   Of course he was furious with me, and threat- ened exposure, but happily I possessed certain letters of his, urging me to expedite my marriage with Mr. Byng, so that if he had exposed me he would have been criminated as well.

' I need not worry you with further details. The story is horrid enough, I know. D'Eyncourt afterwards had some money left him, and ceased to trouble me. You may wonder, considering that I had a good income, why he did not return to me, which he of course might have done openly, by going through the marriage ceremony again. One reason was that he had grown to hate me as cordially as I hated him, and he knew that living together was impossible. After all my experiences, you will hardly wonder that I had a great longing for the love of a good, honest man, whom I could love in return. I found in you one who, I thought, would bring me happiness—one whom I knew I could really love, and who I hoped in time would love me. Deceit had become so completely a part of my nature that I yielded to it again. I felt that at all sacrifices I must win you. You know the rest. I trust one day you will learn to forgive me, for I have been sorely tried and tempted. I still believe that if I had been blessed with a good husband, I should have been a good woman. It was not to be.

'There is one other point I should like to clear up. I never believed that Blanche would marry D'Eyncourt when they were in Italy, although I pretended to think she would. I felt sure her own good sense would keep her safe. I believe, if I had thought otherwise, I would even have sacrificed you to prevent it. You may tell her this one day, although it can make no difference now.'

This, briefly, was Laura Byng's story. If the secrets of all hearts were known, it would not be thought more strange or more sad than a thousand others. Each day brings home to us the fact that truth is far more strange than fiction. The much-abused sensational novelist is the one who depicts life as it really is, not as good people wish it to be.

CHAPTER XLIX.

AN UNEXPECTED VISITOR.

FIRWOLDS was unquestionably a fine estate. You could get to it from a principal station on the South Coast line, from which it was distant about three miles. The road, though good, was somewhat circuitous, and people who knew the district preferred a short-cut of a mile and a half from a little station at which trains stopped but rarely.

This latter road was practicable for horsemen and pedestrians only. It was narrow, and involved the opening of gates here and there, not wide enough for carriages. For about half a mile from the station you followed a lane to a little hamlet. Here, striking into a footpath, you made a descent

across some fields to a stream.   Crossing the
stream by a rustic bridge, you came into
another lane, running at right angles with
the path.   On the opposite side of this lane
was a swing gate, leading into a close coppice,
through which the path to Firwolds ran for
about fifty yards, and then struck across open
fields again for nearly a mile.   After sur-
mounting these fields, for here the ground
sloped upward considerably, you began to
see the tall chimneys of Firwolds above the
tops of the trees which sheltered it from the
south-west gales, and in a few minutes you
reached a gate on the right which opened to
the broad road across the park on the opposite
side of the house to that by which you would
have reached it had you come from the main
station.

If you had your eyes about you when you
passed the gate leading into the coppice
before mentioned, you would have observed
a very quaint old beech-tree, standing only a
yard or two to the right, just within the wood.
It was so old that the trunk had become a
mere tripod, like some of the decayed giants

at Burnham Beeches. You could walk into the trunk from three sides, and find yourself in quite a roomy apartment, or you might lie *perdu* there with your gun, and watch for unwary rabbits, which were so little disturbed in this unfrequented locality that they might be seen by scores in the surrounding fields, and even along the sides of the lane, where the herbage seemed particularly suited to their appetites.

Firwolds House itself lay on an elevated plateau, with a stretch of park land in front. There were some magnificent groups of timber near the house, between which you caught very distant glimpses of the sea, and of purple hills melting away into dim distance. There was a terrace in front of the house, below it a broad sweep of gravel, and a space enclosed by wire fencing, within which were endless beds of crocuses and tulips in the spring, and bright geraniums in the summer. The house itself was modern, built of gray stone, and, though spacious and comfortable, had no particular interest attached to it, as it had only been erected some fifteen years—

that is, soon after Mr. Dalrymple came into the property.

George D'Eyncourt stood upon the terrace in front of the house towards the close of a fine autumn day. He looked out over the broad expanse of park with

'Unelastic lips which seemed to taste possession.'

His brow was serene, his mind at ease, for he had at length attained what he had always looked upon as the *summum bonum* of all earthly good—the possession of Firwolds, with a rent-roll of eight thousand a year.

His uncle was dead and buried, so that, after all the perturbation of spirit the Captain had undergone, things seemed to have fallen into the right groove quite naturally, as far as he was concerned. He knew of nothing that was likely to disturb the serenity of his life, or to interfere with his future plans. Poor Sib Maitland had almost died out of his memory. He had been fond of the girl in his way ; she had been to him

'The summer pilot of an empty heart
Unto the shores of nothing,'

but she had made no sign for some time,
and probably, he argued, had forgotten all
about him by now. Neither did the scurvy
affair of the letters trouble him overmuch.
He was not likely to see anything of the
Lupton party. They would probably fight
shy of him, and he of them, and if the worst
came to the worst, there was no proof against
him. At least, so he argued, for Annette's
careful preservation of the letters was a thing
unknown to him, and as for that wild freak,
the marriage at Sutton-Colville, it was so far
off, and so long ago, that, like the old woman,
he began to think it 'wasn't true.'

D'Eyncourt's steward stood by his side—
that is, at a respectful distance, for the
Captain was not a man who courted fami-
liarity. The steward had grown portly on
the Firwolds estate. Mr. Dalrymple had
left things pretty much in his hands, and he
did not look altogether with favour upon the
younger man now in possession, who seemed
disposed to take the reins himself.

'We must throw out a billiard-room at
that corner, Watson. It is inconceivable

that my uncle overlooked that when the place was built. It is a positive necessity in a country house.'

The Captain pointed to a space between the western side of the house and some magnificent elms, which mingled their broad branches with the chimneys, as if spreading protecting hands over the roof.

'You wouldn't have space enough there, sir, I think. Besides, you would have to cut into the roots of the trees for the foundations.'

'We shall have to cut into the trees themselves, Watson ; they must come down.'

The steward opened his eyes in astonishment.

'Mr. Dalrymple valued those trees greatly, sir. He wouldn't have a branch taken off them.'

'I dare say it won't disturb him now,' said the Captain, with a laugh. 'We must have the billiard-room, and I don't see where else we can put it.'

'The trees are a wonderful ornament to the house, sir,' the steward remonstrated.

'And a billiard-room is a wonderful comfort,' said the Captain. 'I'm not sure we shan't have to take down a good deal of timber—make it pay for the room, in fact. There's too much over yonder on Colt Hill. It cuts off the view. By the way, it would be a great improvement to bring the road past the foot of that hill. It would shorten the distance to the station by half a mile.'

'An expensive job, sir. You would have to cut through the hill to the left.'

'Ah, well, the timber would pay for that, too. There are many things that want looking to. My uncle didn't seem to care much for his surroundings as long as he had a comfortable house. We must go into the question of the rents too. It seems to me that some of the farms are let at a ridiculously low rental. I find, for instance, that White only pays three hundred and fifty pounds for his —a fine farm like that.'

'It's quite as much as he can afford to pay, sir. A great deal of the land is very poor. —not worth ten shillings an acre to farm. He has a hard job to make it pay now.'

' I'm afraid he'll have a still harder job, then, for I'm sure it's worth more than three hundred and fifty pounds, and I mean to get it.   I've gone into these matters lately.'

' He always pays his rent regularly, sir. If you take my advice, you won't interfere with him.   He's got a large family, and I'm sure he can't afford to pay more.'

' That's always the cry.   It's nothing to me whether a man has a large family or not. That's his own look-out.   I want to get what the farm's worth.'

' But he farms well, sir.   He doesn't starve the land.   You won't find a better tenant in all England,' pleaded the steward.

' Ah, well, we'll see.   Suppose you come round to-morrow morning.   Then we can talk over matters generally.'

' Very well, sir.'

' And look here, Watson, I always say what I think.   You've been too easy in these affairs.   I can't go on in the same jog-trot way my uncle did.   You must work in my way in future.   Do you understand ?'

' I suppose I do, sir.   You mean if I don't,

I may look out for another berth,' said the steward with a smile which had something of sarcasm in it.

'That's about what I do mean, Watson. But, mind you, I don't *want* to quarrel. It all depends on yourself. Good-day.'

'Good-day, sir.'

The Captain turned away, and Watson departed, inwardly smothering his wrath. 'A pretty mess he'll make of matters,' he muttered, as soon as he was out of hearing. 'After everything has been going on so comfortably, too,' he added. 'It's hard, confoundedly hard, when a man has done his best for fifteen years, to be upset in all his plans by a conceited jackanapes like that.'

D'Eyncourt took out his cigar-case, and, selecting a cigar, lighted it and proceeded to walk up and down the broad sweep in a still more complacent frame of mind than before.

'I must let these fellows know who's to be master,' he said. 'Nothing like taking a stand at once. It makes matters run quite smoothly afterwards. I think he pretty well understands what sort of man he has to deal with.'

He was interrupted by a step upon the gravel walk. A servant approached from the angle of the house, beyond which was the hall-door.

'If you please, sir, a gentleman wishes to see you,' said the man.

'Who is it?'

'I don't know, sir. He wouldn't give his name. He said he wanted to see you very particularly, sir.'

'Are you sure he is a gentleman?'

'Yes, he seems so, sir.'

'Where is he?'

'In the library, sir.'

D'Eyncourt proceeded to the house and entered the library. As he passed the door, he found himself face to face with Glyn Beverley.

CHAPTER L.

HARD WORDS.

In spite of himself, D'Eyncourt started. Beverley was the very last person he could have expected to see. He recovered himself in a moment, however.

'Beverley, this is an unexpected pleasure,' he said, advancing with outstretched hand.

Glyn stood by the table, but made no movement in response to the Captain's greeting. D'Eyncourt pretended not to notice the slight.

'Won't you take a chair?' he said. 'It is a long time since we met. Shall I offer you a cigar?'

He held out his cigar-case. Glyn put it aside with a hasty movement of his hand.

' Captain D'Eyncourt,' he said, ' it is useless making any pretence of friendliness. I have some grave charges to bring against you. Our interview is not likely to be pleasant to either you or myself.'

' Well, sit down, any way,' said D'Eyncourt, lighting his own cigar, and sinking into an easy-chair. ' It is a pity you won't smoke. It soothes the mind, and might perhaps tend to bring matters to a more amicable issue. Now then, what about these grave charges ?'

Glyn had seated himself near the table, opposite the Captain. He took a note-book from his breast-pocket and selected a paper.

' To begin with,' he said, ' you were guilty of a mean and dastardly action in concocting a letter to which you appended Miss Venables' signature—a forgery, in fact. I will not waste time by dwelling on the consequences of that letter. I merely repeat that in sending it you were guilty of a forgery.'

D'Eyncourt took his cigar from between his lips and looked fixedly at Glyn.

' Look here, Mr. Beverley,' he said ; ' I am

prepared to listen to you as long as you keep a civil tongue in your head. If there is any repetition of such phrases as these, I shall deal with you in another way. I have heard this absurd story about the letter. It is the most ridiculous charge that was ever concocted. If you have come all this way to tell me this, you have taken a great deal of trouble for nothing.'

'You deny having written it?' said Glyn quietly.

'I do, most distinctly.'

Glyn drew from his pocket D'Eyncourt's own letter and placed it in his hand.

'Perhaps that may recall it to your memory,' he said.

For a moment the Captain did not take in the purport of the letter before him. A glance at the first dozen words, however, made him see the trap into which he had fallen. A look of deadly spite flitted across his face. He was not yet, however, at his wits' end.

'Caught, by Jove!' he said with a low laugh. 'You held the trump card there, Beverley, and played it well—deuced well!

But what does it all amount to? All's fair
in love and war, you know. I've done with
war. I played for love.'

'And lost.'

'And lost, I admit; but my loss was your
gain. You got a nice little widow and
eighteen hundred a year, or thereabouts.
What have you to complain of?'

'I'll come to that by-and-by.'

'Oh, take your own time, by all means! But
your last throw was so good, I should not be
disposed to risk another.'

'You'll allow me to be the best judge of
that. We will come now to the question of
the property. You are aware, I suppose,
that I have a claim on it?'

'I've heard some cock-and-bull story about
a will found in a coffin. You had better have
let the old man rest in his grave. You can't
suppose I am going to give up a fine property
like this without fighting. It will involve you
in no end of litigation, and you will probably
lose.'

'I don't think so.'

'No, perhaps not; but possession is nine

points of the law, remember, and I am advised
that you cannot find your witnesses.'

' I don't think they will be necessary.'

' By Jove! they will, though.   You will
have to prove everything.   I tell you what :
I am not in the least afraid of the result, but
I don't mind coming down with something
handsome if you consent to withdraw your
claim.   What do you say, now?   What will
you take ?'

' Nothing.'

Glyn had opened his note-book again, and
was selecting another paper.

' I don't admit your chance, mind,' the
Captain went on.   ' I merely propose this to
save a lot of bother and litigation.   You had
better take advantage of my offer.   I may
not be in the mood to make it again.'   .

' I don't think you will be called on to do
so.   If you do not make terms with me,
the probabilities are that in a week or two
you will find yourself in the clutches of the
law !'

' What the devil do you mean, sir ?'

' Listen to me, Captain D'Eyncourt !   It is

time you heard the truth from someone. You shall hear it from me. You have hitherto escaped with impunity from the consequences of your evil doings. You will escape no longer. Your deceit, your treachery, your lies are at last exposed!'

D'Eyncourt rose from his chair; his eyes flashed fire, and his cheeks were livid with rage.

'By Heaven, sir,' he said, 'you shall pay for this! If you don't instantly leave this house, I will have you kicked out!'

He advanced towards the bell, and placed his fingers upon the handle.

'Stop!' said Glyn, with a face of supreme calm. 'If you ring that bell, it will be the most insane act you ever committed—fatal as far as you are concerned. Let me advise you to return to your chair.'

There was an intense earnestness in Glyn's tone, which absolutely awed the other. He seated himself doggedly.

'Well, I will hear you out,' he said. 'It's a lucky thing for you that you have a patient man to deal with. But be quick. I cannot waste time over this nonsense. What have you got to say?'

'If I could discern one redeeming point in your nature,' Glyn continued, 'I should yet be disposed to spare you in part. I can see none. For mere sport and wantonness you almost broke poor Sib Maitland's heart, and drove her to attempt suicide. You——'

'Stop!' interrupted D'Eyncourt. 'I can't listen to humbug of this sort. You know it is not true. Sib Maitland is as well as ever she was.'

'But for the lucky accident of my meeting her, I tell you, Sib Maitland would have been drowned in the Thames on the night your forged letter arrived.'

'It's a lie!'

'It's the truth, however much you may strive to put it from you. It was I who rescued her.'

'With your usual heroism, I presume,' sneered D'Eyncourt, who was, nevertheless, visibly impressed.

'I will say nothing,' Glyn continued, not heeding the sneer, 'of the deadly injury you

have done me. That, I know, would rather
rejoice you than otherwise. I come now to
another and graver charge. By your vile
arts you won the affection of one of the
purest girls that ever walked this earth.
You sought her in marriage; you would
have married her under circumstances which
you knew, villain as you are, would have
brought ruin and disgrace upon her for life!
Thank Heaven, she discovered your villainy
in time!'

D'Eyncourt started to his feet, his whole
frame quivering with rage. There was a
look of deadly mischief in his eye. He
darted forward, but Glyn was too quick for
him, for the next moment he had him by the
collar, and was forcing him down into his
chair.

'You scoundrel!' said Glyn, with sup-
pressed rage. 'If you attempt violence,
I will have no mercy on you. I am not
likely to have much patience with a man who
has connived at bigamy!'

A quick gasp escaped from D'Eyncourt's
lips as the last word was uttered.

'Take off your hands!' he said. 'You have the advantage of inches, confound you! Now, tell me what you mean by bigamy. This is another of your lies, I suppose?'

'I am not likely to face such a man as you without proof,' said Glyn. 'You will not deny this, I suppose?'

He held out another paper. D'Eyncourt glanced at it, and as he did so his lips grew livid, and his whole frame seemed to collapse. It was a copy of the marriage register in Sutton-Colville Church.

'Damnation!'

The word came like a savage growl. D'Eyncourt saw that the game was up. He threw himself back in his chair with an evil scowl and clenched fists. Presently he looked at Glyn.

'You have the best of the game, I admit,' he said. 'But why do you come here to tell me all this? Why not let the law take its course?'

'I do not come to screen you; of that you may be sure,' Glyn answered. 'You deserve the worst punishment the law could inflict;

but I wish, as far as possible, to avoid publicity. If you choose to depart before I institute proceedings, you can go. My course will then be comparatively clear. Your wife is already gone.'

' Where ?'

' To America.'

' And you would advise my following her?'

' That is a matter entirely for your own consideration. For her sake, I should not advise it.'

The Captain paused, as if reflecting. Suddenly a strange expression flitted across his face. He looked up.

' The situation, I take it, is this,' he said. ' If I don't clear out and give up the property, you not only put in your claim, but you charge me with conniving at bigamy.'

' That is precisely what I shall do.'

' Exactly. It is an ugly situation for a man of my position. But even if the law can touch me, which is doubtful, I might still fight for the property.'

' Which you would not have the slightest chance of retaining.'

'That is a matter of opinion. However, the question is worth considering. I confess I don't care for the exposure. Will you give me a week to decide?'

'I will not give you a day. I must have your decision now.'

Again the strange expression came into the Captain's face—a look of a sudden resolve.

'You drive a hard bargain,' he said. 'However, as I don't care for the risk and exposure, I will go. I suppose,' he added with a sardonic grin, 'you won't object to a tip now and then if a poor devil is hard up?'

'That will depend entirely on circumstances,' said Glyn.

'Exactly so. You will do the magnanimous if I behave myself. Well, I will try. And now, while I am yet in possession, let me offer you the hospitalities of Firwolds. What will you take?'

'Nothing, thank you. My business is over. I am anxious to get back as soon as possible.'

'I will not detain you, but I am sorry you

won't have anything.   Shall I order your trap?'

'Thanks, I am walking.'

D'Eyncourt looked up quickly.

'By the short-cut?' he said.

'Yes.'

'How on earth did you find your way?'

'By dint of inquiry at the village.   It is not difficult.'

'And you won't let me send you back?'

'No thanks; I prefer walking.'

'As you will.'

They proceeded together to the hall-door. D'Eyncourt looked up at the sky.

'There is a storm brewing,' he said. 'You had better accept my offer.'

'I shall be at the station before it breaks.'

'I hope you will.   I presume, then, we shall not meet again.   By the way,' he added with the same sardonic smile, 'you have not yet told me when you expect me to clear out.'

'Within a month at the most,' answered Glyn briefly.

He walked away at a quick pace down the drive leading to the footway across the fields.

He was revolving in his mind D'Eyncourt's sudden surrender. What did it mean? What was the meaning of the covert look of triumph which accompanied his submission? Was he contemplating some new devilry? In spite of himself, Glyn felt uneasy.

D'Eyncourt stood gazing after him until he was out of sight. Then he turned and entered the house.

As he did so a low growl of thunder broke from a bank of clouds beyond the fields through which Glyn's path lay.

CHAPTER LI.

D'EYNCOURT went direct to his smoking-room. The walls of this room were ornamented with quite an unusual display of whips, sticks, weapons, pipes, foxes' heads and tails, horns of various animals, and the hundred-and-one things which men of a roving disposition collect as reminiscences of their various travels and exploits. Among these articles was a short instrument with a heavily weighted knob at one end and a leather thong for the wrist at the other. It was about a foot in length, with a thin flexible handle. The knob, which was weighted with lead, was so heavy that in an unscrupulous hand it might become an absolutely murderous weapon. Yet by a singular contradiction of terms it was called a 'life-preserver.'

D'Eyncourt took this down from its hook, placed it within the inner breast-pocket of his coat and buttoned his coat over it. Then he went to the hall, and, opening a closet in which was a collection of coats and hats, he selected a thin waterproof, which he threw over his arm, and, putting on a round felt hat, he returned to the back of the house and passed out in the direction of the stables.

Although he was perfectly calm, there was a quickness of movement in all this which was somewhat unusual with him. He stopped, however, when he reached the gate leading to the stable-yard. An idea seemed to strike him, and he passed the gate with his usual deliberation. An under-groom was passing into the stable with a bundle of litter.

' I'm thinking of riding over to Brighton, Clark,' said the Captain. ' I don't quite like the look of the weather.'

The man glanced up at the sky. The low

bank of cloud before mentioned was hidden by the house.   Except for some driving scud, the sky above was clear.

'I don't think it will be much, sir.   We might have a shower or two.'

'Put the saddle on Bobby then—or stay, what condition is Kitty in?   Has she been at any of her pranks lately?'

They had entered the stable.   Kitty was in a stall a little to the right.   She gave one of her usual backward glances as D'Eyncourt entered, a glance that boded mischief.

'I have not ridden the mare since my uncle's death, I believe,' said D'Eyncourt. 'She would carry me quicker than Bobby if she's in a decent temper.   Can you saddle her?'

The man hesitated.   To do Kitty justice, she held them all in awe.   D'Eyncourt read the man's thoughts.

'Call Green, then,' he said—'or stay; give me the saddle; I'll do it myself.'

The groom brought a saddle from the harness-room, and held it ready for his master.   D'Eyncourt walked boldly into the stall, and, with a firm hand, unbuckled the roller which held the horse-cloth.

Kitty hated a coward. If D'Eyncourt had hesitated, the probabilities are that there would have been a scene. As it was, she simply watched the proceedings out of the corner of her eye.

The cloth was stripped, and the saddle on in half a minute. As D'Eyncourt tightened the girths, the mare laid back her ears flat on to her crest, but she did not resist. The groom was ready with the bridle: D'Eyncourt took it in his hand.

'Not that. Green doesn't ride her with a Pelham, does he? I've said over and over again she goes quieter with a snaffle.'

'I believe he's afraid of her with a snaffle, sir,' said the man, with a sickly grin.   •

'Stuff and nonsense! Why can't he take my advice? Nothing irritates her like a curb-chain.'

'He says he can't hold her with a snaffle, sir.'

'No; because he's always worrying her mouth, I suppose. If he let her have her

head, she'd be as quiet as a lamb. Get a
plain snaffle.'

In the few moments the man was absent,
D'Eyncourt slipped off the halter, and passed
his hand caressingly down Kitty's nose. For
a wonder the mare responded, and arched
her neck in evident satisfaction. The next
moment the bridle was brought, the reins
thrown over the mare's neck, and the bit
slipped in between her teeth without a
struggle.

Kitty was certainly a magnificent specimen
of horseflesh. Although he knew her so
thoroughly, D'Eyncourt could not help running his eyes once more over her splendid
points, and looking with inward satisfaction
on the long elastic step, as she came from
the stable.

The action of saddling seemed to have
diverted his thoughts a moment ; but as he
approached the side of the mare, a dark, fixed
look came into his face. He glanced up at
the sky once more.

'If the weather should turn out very bad,
I shall stay the night, Clark. By the way,

send into the house at once, and say I am not likely to be home to dinner. Don't let them keep it after eight. Let go her head ; it only fidgets her.'

He had the reins in his hand, and his foot in the stirrup. Kitty and her master were evidently on better terms than they were when we first made their acquaintance. She let him mount without a struggle.

Then D'Eyncourt passed out of the stable yard at a steady walk.

Although chafing with a horrible impatience, he continued the easy pace until he had turned the angle of the drive which hid him from view. He knew that the groom was probably watching him. He was right. The man stood at the gate, gazing after him in amazement.

'By Jingo, he's a cool hand ; I believe he's the devil himself ! Green would have had the mare all over the shop before he'd a-mounted her,' he said, as he shut the gate and returned to the stable.

Once out of sight, Kitty seemed to read her master's thoughts. Without any sign from him, except that mysterious communication between a good rider and his horse, she broke into a canter, and was at the outer park gate in a few seconds. The lodge-keeper's wife hurried out to open the gate.

'Good-evening, Mrs. Bond.   Likely to have some rain, I think.'

'It looks like it, sir.'

'Is your husband better?'

'Yes, sir, thank you.   He's getting nicely again now.'

'He must be more careful with those machines.   He might have taken his hand off.'

'Yes, sir.   It's well he escaped as he did.'

A hundred yards from the lodge, a road diverged to the left.   This was the direct route to Shoreham.   D'Eyncourt pulled up at this point, and looked cautiously around. There was not a soul visible.   The evening was closing in.   A few drops of rain fell upon the dusty road, leaving splashes as large as a penny piece.   To his right was a high bank, with a low, stunted hedge on the top, and beyond it a broad stretch of grazing-land, with some cattle intent upon their evening meal. Beyond this, again, was a wooden fence, and then the ground dropped to the valley, in which lay the stream which Glyn had to cross on his way back to the station. The distance to this stream and the coppice opposite was about a mile as the crow flies.

'Nine miles to Brighton,' mused D'Eyncourt, as he sat motionless on his mare. 'If I take the short-cut over the downs, and go into the old Shoreham lane, I ought to do it in three-quarters of an hour; going easy by the road, an hour and a quarter. Kitty will give me the spare half-hour, I fancy.'

Another look around. Still not a soul visible. Only the tinkle of a sheep-bell to the left, and the crop-crop of the cattle pulling at the rich grass in the field. Without another thought, D'Eyncourt put Kitty at the bank, and lifted her over in splendid style. The next moment he was crossing the field, amid the startled cattle, at racing speed.

Kitty took the low fence beyond the field almost in her stride, then she went away down the grass slope at the same headlong speed.   There was a thick wood at the bottom of this slope—a preserve, in fact—which extended for a mile or more in the direction of the station towards which Glyn was wending his way.   Through this preserve was a broad path used only by people belonging to the estate, and that very rarely. D'Eyncourt knew it to be a most unfrequented spot.   It was in the last degree unlikely that he would meet anyone there at that hour.

As he reached the depths of the wood, still going as fast as the rough road would permit, it grew almost dark.   The gloom was increased by the dense leafage overhead, and the thickly gathering clouds.   Suddenly a vivid flash of lightning broke right in front, followed by a crash of thunder which seemed to shake the ground.   Then came a flood of rain like a second deluge.   Kitty swerved a moment, but D'Eyncourt put his hand on her neck caressingly and lightly touched her with his heel. She responded by plunging swiftly on through the darkness.

'If she keeps her temper to-night she shall live in clover for the rest of her days,' muttered the Captain.

Another flash even more vivid than the last broke from the clouds. Then came another crash and another deluge. D'Eyncourt gave a low laugh.

'This is about the best thing that could happen,' he said. 'The very elements favour me. Poor devil! he must be soaked by this time.'

In another three minutes he drew rein.

'It must be somewhere about here,' he said. 'Another flash would show me.'

As he spoke the lightning again leaped from the clouds. He was clear of the wood by this time, and the sudden illumination showed him a shed standing a little to the right on the skirts of the wood. He rode towards it.

It was a sort of rude cattle-shed with cob

walls and a roof of rough thatch.   The
wooden door hung loosely on its hinges.

D'Eyncourt swung it open and led Kitty
in.   The mare shook herself free from the
moisture which streamed down her coat, and
seemed to like the shelter.

'She takes kindly to it.   She will be quiet
here, no doubt.   I may risk it for ten
minutes, any way.'

He patted Kitty's neck and said a sooth-
ing word or two.   Then he passed out of the
shed and closed the door behind him.   The
fastening of the door was gone.

He looked about for some way to secure it.
There was a balk of timber lying against
the side of the shed.   D'Eyncourt drew it
across the door.

'That will keep it.   She will not be
anxious to get outside in this weather.
Good God, what a deluge!'

He passed quickly across the open space
in which the hut stood.   On the other side
of it was a flight of hurdles, and then the
coppice through which Glyn had to pass.

Springing over the hurdles, he passed into the coppice. Struggling as quickly as he could through the tangled undergrowth amid the saplings, he reached the old beech-tree which stood near the swing-gate. Here he paused a moment and listened.

There was no sound save the heavy pattering of the rain upon the leaves and an occasional low growl of thunder overhead. Had the storm ceased, or was it gathering for a fresh effort?

The clouds had cleared somewhat in the western sky, and there was a dull light issuing from below their heavy fringes—the last lurid gleam of the dying day.

D'Eyncourt took out his watch. He could just discern the face.

'He cannot have passed,' he said. 'I have come by a shorter cut, and he is on foot. No; I must be in time.'

He stepped back into the hollow of the beech-tree and drew the life-preserver from his breast-pocket. He gave another low laugh as he poised it in his hand.

'You should be called by a new name after to-night,' he said.   'You will be as good as eight thousand a year to me, my trusty friend.'

He drew closely within the hollow of the tree and stood there listening.

CHAPTER LII.

A THUNDERSTORM.

WHEN Glyn left Firwolds, he strode away down the drive at a rapid pace. On reaching the gate which led into the path across the fields, however, he slackened speed and took out his watch.

'It is useless hurrying,' he said. 'I have nearly an hour, and I can walk it easily in half that time.'

He had gained his point with D'Eyncourt; but, for all that, he was not in a happy frame of mind. He had been so mixed up with a long course of deceit and crime that a sort of taint seemed to have settled upon himself. At least, this was his sensation at the moment.

'If I could only wash myself free of it all, and feel more worthy of her!' he cried. 'Linked as I have been, and still am, with that woman, I dare not even approach her. When I am quite free I shall still have the taint of sin about me. I could never ask her to degrade herself by marrying me. Nothing but perfect purity should be associated with her. I have been defiled in spite of myself. It is the curse of Cain, I suppose.'

He spoke and felt bitterly. The experience of the last year had taken all life and hope out of him. He was rapidly becoming a confirmed pessimist. What was the use of this constant struggle with fate? Life was not worth living with the present cloud over him.

All this, of course, meant that life was not worth living without Blanche. That was the secret of it. Now that a fortune was within his grasp, he did not value it, for it could not be shared with her. He rather turned from the thought with loathing. After all, he was not sure that he had taken the wisest course.

Perhaps it would have been better to have
left Laura and D'Eyncourt to pursue their
evil courses unmolested. His own life would
only be the worse for the exposure. It would
have been better to have left the country,
and worked out a career for himself in
another land.

Some heavy drops of rain interrupted his
musings. He looked up at the sky. Dark
clouds had gathered overhead. A storm was
evidently about to break.

The day had been unusually fine. He
had left his overcoat and umbrella at the
station, not wishing to be encumbered with
them in his walk.

'It doesn't much matter if I get a soaking,'
he said. 'I may just as well stay at Worthing
for the night, and see Norwood in the
morning.

He walked on more briskly, nevertheless.
One does not usually saunter with the prospect
of exposure to a heavy storm. He had
reached the last field but one on the Firwolds
side of the coppice, when the first vivid flash
of lightning broke from the clouds, and the

rain came down in a terrific flood. There
was a clump of elms just off the path. Glyn
stepped under them for shelter.

'It is so heavy that I think it will soon
pass,' he said.

A deafening crash of thunder broke over
his head, and then as suddenly ceased. Then
there was a lull of a few seconds before the
flood came down. A strange stillness for a
moment prevailed.

The sound of a horse's hoofs, proceeding
at a rapid pace, struck on Glyn's ear.

'Somebody riding hard for shelter,' he
said.

Another vivid flash, another thunder peal,
and then more rain. The clouds were piled
like ramparts of lead above. Darkness had
settled down upon the earth.

'I can't stop here,' said Glyn. 'It seems
to grow worse and worse. I may as well
get a soaking in the open as under these
trees, and I may miss my train.'

He emerged from the shelter into the wild
storm. Buttoning his coat tightly about him,
and with his hat set well down on his fore-

head, he faced the rain and the vivid lightning, which now came in almost constant flashes.   Blinded and dazzled, he opened the gate leading into the coppice, and pressed on between the young trees.

He reached the gate on the further side, and pushed it open.   His hand was still upon it, when there came another lull in the storm.   Glyn looked up at the sky.

It was his last look at God's heaven.   As he raised his eyes, a ragged gleam of lightning, intense and beautiful, leaped from the cloud right above.

A sharp pang, as of hot iron, scorched his eyes, and darted through his frame.   He staggered forward through the gateway, and across the path.   There was a drop of a foot or two into the road below.   In another instant Glyn had fallen lifeless on to the ragged stones in the roadway, cutting his temple severely as he fell.

D'Eyncourt stole out of the wood, and through the gateway, weapon in hand.   He paused in amazement as he saw the prostrate figure in the road below.

The next moment he was down beside his intended victim, with his arm upraised to strike.

Something in the absolute stillness of the form arrested his hand. He turned the lifeless figure over, face upwards. The face was livid and motionless, and there was a great gash in the forehead, from which the blood was flowing.

Even D'Eyncourt was staggered.

'This is death,' he said. 'Either the fall or the lightning has saved me the trouble.'

He picked up his life-preserver, which he had let fall by the stricken man's side. At that moment a sound broke on his ear. He hastily thrust the life-preserver inside his coat, not noticing that it was stained with the blood which flowed from Glyn's temple. Then he stood still and listened.

CHAPTER LIII.

A SOUND of rapidly approaching wheels.

D'Eyncourt had no time to spare. He hastily retreated into the copse, and sought the shelter of the old tree.

'A cursed chance!' he said. 'I hoped to have got clear away. I think he is pretty well finished, however.'

Then a great trembling seized him. He had passed the barrier which shut him out from communion and sympathy with his fellow-men for evermore. But for the intervention of the elements, he would now be a murderer!

'What nonsense is this?' he muttered. 'I shall spoil all if I give way.'

He crouched within the tree and listened.
The wheels came rapidly on, and he heard
voices. Now they were close at hand.

'What the dickens is that?' said a voice.

The sound of wheels ceased. The vehicle
had come to a stop.

'What do you mean, Jim?' said another
voice.

'Why, there—don't you see it? Is he
drunk or dead? Jump out and see.'

There was a creaking sound as of a descent
from a vehicle, then footsteps, then a voice
of alarm.

'My God, Jim! this is a bad affair. Here's
a man covered with blood. Jump out, quick!
the mare will stand.'

The sound of someone else alighting,
then another startled exclamation.

'Is he dead?'

'I think so. This is an ugly business.'

'What's to be done?'

'God knows.'

'Lift him up a bit, poor devil! It's all
over with him, I fancy.'

'A gentleman, too, seemingly. Is his watch gone?'

'No, but he's been hit in the forehead. Jim, this looks like murder!'

A pause of a moment, then a lower tone.

'I say, the fellow may be about.'

'Not he. Whoever he is, he wouldn't stop for our coming. Besides, we don't know how long he has lain here.'

'He's not cold.'

'By George! no more he is.'

'We must take him into the cart. It's precious lucky you were with me. There may be life in him yet.'

'We must mark the bearings, then. There will be no end of a business about this. See here; it is right opposite that gate. He has come that way, I expect.'

'Where does the path lead to?'

'Firwolds — Mr. Dalrymple's place—or, rather, Captain D'Eyncourt's.'

'Well, don't let us stand talking here. There may be a chance for the poor chap Now then, gently. Stop; let down the tail-board first.'

A sound of a pin withdrawn, and the rattle of a chain.

'Now then; take him gently by the feet. I've got his shoulders. Steady, lass—wo, ho!'

'Let him lie so. I can keep his head against my knee. We'll throw the rug over him.'

'Where are we to take him ?'

'I never thought of that. It's a long way to the station. Firwolds is the nearest house.'

'Can we take him there ?'

'They can't refuse in a case like this. Besides, they can send a man on horseback for a doctor.'

'Ain't the village nearer?'

'Across the fields it is, but we can't drive that way. It's double the distance round by the road. No, Firwolds is the place. Have you got him right?'

'As right as I can. Drive on easy.'

The horse went on again at a steady trot, and Glyn Beverley went to the home of his ancestors—feet first.

D'Eyncourt stole from his hiding-place.

He had never thought to pass through such
a five minutes as this last.   Every word he
had heard had struck him with a deadly chill,
and there was a strange mockery of fate in
the destination of his victim.

'If it should bring the affair home to me!'
he groaned.

Then he braced up his nerves.   'It won't
do to give way like this,' he said.   'Kitty
must save me.   If I am in Brighton in half
an hour or so, they cannot possibly suspect
me.   They noticed he was not cold.'

He leaped desperately through the undergrowth towards the clearing.   In three
seconds he had reached the fence, and was
running at full speed towards the shed.

All was as he had left it, Kitty still standing quietly within, her head down as if
dozing.

'So much the better,' said D'Eyncourt,
'considering what she has to do.'

Had Kitty, like her master, entered into
a league with Satan, that she lent herself
so completely to these evil deeds ?   It
seemed so.

D'Eyncourt mounted and turned his horse in the direction of the wood through which he had come from Firwolds. Then he drew rein a moment.

'No, it will not do to risk the fences in the dark. I must take the short-cut over the downs,' he said.

He turned into the road through a gate, and, following it for a quarter of a mile or so, reached the skirts of some open downs which stretched away in the direction he wished to go. For a mile or more it was fair galloping ground, with not a fence nor a hedge to impede his progress.

'There is only the old chalk-pit,' he said. 'If I edge away well to the left, I may keep her at speed across here. It will save a mile. She can do it by this light. It is all plain sailing.'

Kitty's placid mood had made him forgetful of her temper. He touched her somewhat suddenly with his heel. The mare gave a bound which would have unseated a less skilful rider. Then she went off at full speed.

'More rain,' said D'Eyncourt. 'I thought it was going to clear. Instead of that it seems coming up thicker than ever. No matter; it will wash the sweat off the mare and prevent suspicion. I wonder what they will do with *him* when they get him to Firwolds.'

Kitty had settled down into her stride by this time, and was going like the wind. D'Eyncourt, as if by the exercise of his will, had urged her to her utmost speed. The black ground seemed to fly beneath her feet.

Dark night now, and blinding rain, and a moaning wind from off the sea.

'Confound it! this is almost too much of a good thing. It is not a night I should choose for a gallop across the downs, but needs must when the devil drives, and I must be in the town in half an hour.'

A deep depression in the downs, and then another rise to a windy hill-top. Up hill or down, there was no change in the mare's even, monotonous stride.

'I must edge away more to the left. It is so infernally dark it is impossible to see a dozen yards.   We are going too near the pit.'

A gentle pressure on the left rein, which was not responded to.   A still stronger pull. The mare went on, straight.

'Come, Kitty, don't be obstinate after your good behaviour,' said D'Eyncourt, squaring his reins and making a decided effort to keep the mare to the left.   'What the devil does the brute mean?' he added, still finding his efforts vain.

Kitty meant going straight.   Not an inch did her head budge in response to the pressure.   There was only a slight quickening of her pace, which was now tremendous.

'This won't do.   The brute is going dead on to the chalk-pit, I do believe.'

He rose in his stirrups, took the reins in a still firmer grasp with both hands, and made one decided effort to get the mare in hand. He might as well have tried to turn an avalanche.

She had taken the bit between her teeth. With her head down, she plunged on through the darkness, utterly unmoved by his efforts.

One frantic attempt to pull her up. His strength drew her head in close to her chest; but there was no diminution of her speed. If anything, she seemed to pull herself together and increase it—a mad plunging pace over which D'Eyncourt had no more influence than a child.

'Good God! The pit!'

He saw it looming dimly right before him. The ragged edge—beyond which nothing was visible but mist and darkness.

It was maddening! He tugged and sawed at the reins like a man possessed. Kitty had been obedient long enough. She would have her own way now.

It was not half a dozen strides away—that dark ragged edge. A deadly chill struck D'Eyncourt's heart. A creeping horror seemed to lift his hair at the roots. With a wild yell he dropped the reins, and the next moment threw himself clear from the saddle.

As he thought. But, like the irresistible clutch of Fate, the stirrup iron gripped his foot and dragged him onward head downward.

But even before the life was knocked out
of him they were on the brink. There was
a loud snort of terror on the very edge, and
a frantic struggle to check the mad career.
It was too late. A wild pawing of the air
for a brief space, and then horse and man
went headlong to the depths below.

Late the next afternoon, when the storm
had all passed and the level sun lay warm
upon the short grass, a boy in charge of
cattle sauntered to the edge of the old chalk-
pit and looked below.

At first he hardly realized what he saw,
but presently it dawned upon him in all its
horror. A dead horse lay beneath, with its
neck broken, and doubled up beside it, in a
shapeless heap, lay a dead man.

CHAPTER LIV.

'I CANNOT imagine why Glyn doesn't write. I fear he must be sadly bothered,' said Kate, as she and Blanche were sitting at breakfast.

'She may still be giving him trouble. She may refuse to go at the last moment. It is a terrible business.'

'She can hardly do that. Think what the alternative would be!'

'But she may trust to your brother's forbearance. She may think, rather than push matters to an extreme, he would leave her in peace.'

'She could never think he would countenance such a vile act as she has been guilty of, and make a victim of himself for life.'

'It is hardly conceivable, but she might. There is no knowing what wild fancies may fill a woman's mind when driven to such a strait.   How little I dreamed of all this, when she used to be here so much!   It is dreadful even to have known such a woman.'

'And yet at the outset she may have been more sinned against than sinning.'

'Let us hope so.   Still, there was no excuse for her when she was her own mistress.'

'But people get so hardened in crime, especially when they escape with impunity from one offence after another.   Detection is the last thing that seems to occur to them.   Give me the newspaper while you read your letters.   What heaps you always have!'

'Most of them begging ones, I am sorry to say.   One of the penalties of wealth is the daily perusal of endless tales of woe.   Really, it quite saddens one's life without any troubles of one's own.'

Blanche proceeded to open her letters, while Kate read the evening paper of the

day before. They had not been thus em-
ployed for more than five minutes when there
was a startled exclamation from Kate.

'Oh, Blanche! what is this?'

Blanche looked up. The expression of
her friend's face terrified her. She was by
her side in a moment, and this is what they
both saw:

'With reference to the shocking occurrence narrated in our issue of this morning,
our Sussex correspondent telegraphs that a
further discovery has been made which lends
additional horror to the tragedy which has
been enacted. The day after the discovery
of the almost lifeless body of Mr. Glyn
Beverley, a boy happened to be wandering
along the edge of an old chalk-pit, within a
mile of the place where the assault was committed. On looking down he perceived some
strange objects lying at the bottom. He
made his way down as quickly as possible,
and found that the objects which had attracted
his attention were the dead bodies of a man
and horse, which had evidently fallen over

the cliff. The boy immediately gave the alarm, and some men from a neighbouring farm hastened to the spot. It has been ascertained that the body of the man is that of Captain D'Eyncourt, who has recently succeeded to his uncle's property in that neighbourhood, and to whose house Mr. Beverley was carried on the night of the fatal occurrence. The whole affair is at present enveloped in mystery, but the matter has caused the greatest excitement in the neighbourhood, and the police are making active inquiries.'

With arms clasped about each other, the two girls read this terrible paragraph. There was no blinking the facts. They were before them in black and white, narrated in the cold, business-like style of a newspaper correspondent.

They had hardly realized what they saw, when the door opened suddenly, and the Vicar entered the room. He took in the situation at once.

'My dear girls, I was so hoping to be in

time,' he said, advancing, and taking the paper from their hands.

Kate was the first to speak.

'Oh, Mr. Dyke! is he alive?' she cried.

'Yes, dear child; by the latest accounts, most assuredly. I was so hoping to be here before you saw the papers; but there is another dreadful thing for which you must be prepared.'

'We know what you mean — Captain D'Eyncourt. It is all too terrible,' said Kate.

They were both inwardly thanking God, nevertheless, that Glyn was alive.

Little by little—for it was difficult to realize the dreadful story at once—they began to grasp the full meaning of all the Vicar told them. How that Glyn had been found by two farmers in a lane near Firwolds, with a frightful wound in his forehead. How he had been taken in their light trap to the house he had just left, and from which the owner, Captain D'Eyncourt, was then absent. How that he still remained unconscious, but that the doctor who had been summoned had expressed a hope that his injuries were not absolutely of a fatal character.   How that, following on the account of the outrage, came the intelligence of the discovery of D'Eyncourt's body, and the wild rumours to which the discovery gave rise.

But there was one fact which not even the Vicar was yet aware of—a damning fact which linked D'Eyncourt incontestably with what appeared like a murderous assault on Glyn.   In the breast-pocket of his coat was found a weapon covered with blood, which, in the opinion of the doctors, might have inflicted a wound like the one on luckless Glyn's forehead.

London was already ringing with the account of this new discovery which appeared in the morning papers, and in a few hours the news would reach Harleyford itself, and Blanche and her friend would have to bear the shock of this new horror in the tragedy with which they were so closely connected.

By-and-by came a telegram from Mr. Norwood, who had, of course, been startled by the dreadful news that was agitating the

district. He had gone at once to Firwolds,
and found Glyn still unconscious. Although
the doctor was somewhat hopeful, he ad-
mitted that the present condition of the
sufferer was most critical, and begged Mr.
Norwood to communicate without delay with
his friends. So Kate was sent for, and
entreated to come at once.

It was only by a great effort they could
maintain sufficient calm to make the necessary
preparations. The first violence of the shock
over, Kate became more collected than her
friend, for Blanche, strive as she might, could
not shut out the fact that the life of the man
she loved was in danger—that she might not,
in fact, see him again alive. In the presence
of this fear all considerations were cast aside.

They were on the point of departure, when
another telegram arrived.

'Sibyl will be with you by the 12.30 train
to-day. She is very ill. Pray meet her at
station.'

This was from Sib's father. Here was a
new complication. It had all been so

arranged by Blanche herself, but the dreadful shock of the morning had driven it from her mind.

'What is to be done?' said Blanche, in utter bewilderment. 'I must meet her, poor girl!'

'Blanche dear, I think it is better so. It seems cruel to say it, but I have felt from the first it would be wiser for me to go alone. Think what it would be to you to see poor Glyn in this condition, darling.'

'Oh, Kate, Kate, you do not know the horrid fear that possesses me. If he should die, and I should not see him again!'

She sank into a chair, with hands clasped before her in speechless anguish. Kate knelt at her side, and put her arms round her.

'No, no, Blanche. It cannot, must not be. We will not anticipate this. At least, let me see him before you come. Believe me, darling, it is better. I will send a telegram the moment I have seen him, and if danger is imminent, which God forbid, I will tell you to come. No doubt Mrs. Dyke would stay with Sib.'

And then a new fear rushed into their minds. If Sib should see the news in the evening papers, it would almost kill her. What were the chances? It was evident the news had not reached her home when her father sent the telegram. Would she hear of it on the way? A maid was to come with her, and they were to have a reserved compartment. This Blanche had arranged, for Sib had been getting worse and worse, and was coming in order that she might receive proper care and nursing, which Blanche knew was almost impossible in her home. The chances were they would not think of newspapers on the way, and there would be no gossips in the carriage with them.

This thought, however, decided Blanche. The fatal news must be kept from Sib at all hazards. With a terrible aching of heart she abandoned the idea of going with Kate.

'But, Kate, you will promise me most solemnly that you will send for me if there is immediate danger.'

'I promise most solemnly, darling.'

So Kate went on her sad journey in company with the Vicar, who at the last moment had proposed to accompany her and bring back news of the sufferer. This was a great relief to all.

Mrs. Dyke went with Blanche to meet poor Sib. The meeting was another shock, for the girl looked stricken with death, and Blanche had need of all her fortitude to bear up under this new complication.

As to the cause of the murderous attack on Glyn, as it was supposed to be, the whole party lost themselves in vain conjectures, for the news had not yet arrived of the discovery of the weapon in D'Eyncourt's possession. When that fact became known, it fixed the guilt at once on him. No other theory, indeed, was started. The simple fact that Glyn was found lying face upward convinced the startled world that it was no accident, and that D'Eyncourt was guilty. As, indeed, morally speaking, he was.

CHAPTER LV.

BROKEN DOWN.

THE Vicar had telegraphed to Mr. Norwood to say they were coming, so a carriage was waiting for them at the station. Mr. Norwood had taken upon himself the charge of the injured man until his sister arrived.

He met them in the hall at Firwolds. Kate was too much overcome to speak.

' How is he now?' asked the Vicar.

' The surgeon from London is now.with him. We must be patient for a short time. Miss Beverley, we meet under painful circumstances. Let me beg of you to bear up. I have reason to think the doctors are more hopeful.'

' Is he still unconscious?' asked Kate, through her tears.

'Yes, but they think it is merely con-
cussion, not a fracture.   Let us hope for the
best.   There is a friend of your brother's in
the drawing-room.   He would not intrude
on you until he knew whether you would like
to see him.'

'Who is it?'

'A Mr. Forbes.   He came at once on
hearing of the accident, and has been most
kind and useful.'

Through all her wretchedness and anxiety,
a little glow of pleasure stole over Kate's
heart as she heard the name.   She seemed
in some indefinite way to find relief in the
thought that Forbes was near her.

'It is indeed kind of him.   Certainly, I
will see him at once.'

She proceeded to the drawing-room.
Forbes heard and recognised her footstep.
He stood near the door, looking quite shy
and awkward.

'How good of you to come!' Kate said as
she shook hands.

'I was afraid I might be in the way, don't
you know,' Forbes answered with a downcast

look. 'I like Beverley so much, I couldn't stay away when I heard of the affair, but I left it to you whether to see me or not. I shall leave it to you to tell me candidly if I am in the way; but if I can be of any use, I shall be delighted to ride over every day, don't you know.'

'I cannot give you so much trouble as that; but since you are so kind, I must say it is quite a relief to me to think you are here. It is at a time like this that one finds out the real value of one's friends.'

'Then, if it is any relief to you, you must really let me come every day. It is not the least trouble, I assure you.'

Forbes purposely abstained from any mention of D'Eyncourt. Things were bad enough without referring to such diabolical wickedness, and Forbes' mission in life seemed to be to make everyone with whom he came in contact as happy as the circumstances would admit.

The Vicar and Mr. Norwood, who had remained behind for a little confidential chat,

now entered the room.   Kate went to take
off her things.

'I am extremely glad to find you here,
Forbes,' the Vicar said.   'Are you staying
in the neighbourhood?'

'About fifteen miles off.   I have ridden
over this morning.'

'I wish you were in the house.   You would
be a great help to that poor girl while her
brother is in this critical state.'

'Well, it wouldn't exactly do, don't you
know; but I can ride over often.   I thought
Blanche Venables would be here.'

'She could not come on account of her
cousin, who is very ill.'

'What, Sib Maitland?'

'Yes; very ill indeed, I believe.'

'I'm awfully sorry to hear it.   There
seems to be no end to their troubles.'

The great surgeon who had been sent for
by Mr. Norwood here entered the room with
the local practitioner.

'What about your patient, Sir James?'
asked the lawyer.

'In one respect a very good report.   There

is no fracture, and he has recovered consciousness; but we have made a very sad
discovery.'

'What is that?'

'Whether from the effects of the blow or
what we do not know, but he is quite blind.'

'Blind!' echoed all in amazement.

'Yes.   There are certain tree-marks about
the body which indicate lightning.   I am
told there was a very violent storm here the
night the outrage was committed.   It seems
a strange coincidence, but I think it must
have been the lightning.'

'It is a very dreadful thing,' said Mr.
Norwood.

'How on earth shall we break it to his
sister?' said Forbes.

'She knows it already,' said the surgeon.
'It was useless keeping it from her.   I have
led her to believe, as I myself hope, that it is
only temporary.   But we must not be too
sanguine.'

'Is she with her brother?'

'No, I have begged her not to go to him
just at present.   He must be kept perfectly

quiet. The nurse seems very efficient, and
has my instructions. You will send for me
again if necessary ; meanwhile Mr. Melluish
will doubtless do all that is required.'

The great man took his departure. The
Vicar went to comfort Kate, while Mr. Norwood and Forbes passed the time as best
they could under the circumstances. They
decided to stay until the meeting between
the brother and sister was over, so that they
might take away the latest report.

By-and-by the Vicar returned.

' Miss Beverley has begged me to stay at
any rate until to-morrow,' he said. ' I don't
like to refuse her. Would you undertake to
convey a message to Miss Venables ? It is
giving you a great deal of trouble.'

' Don't think of that I shall be only too
glad to go.'

' It is very good of you. A personal
report will be so much more satisfactory than
a telegram. I don't know what to do about
mentioning the blindness. It will be only
needlessly distressing her.'

' I don't think it worth while to say any-

thing about it.   He may recover from it,'
said Mr. Norwood.

'Well, well, let us suppress the fact for the
present.   She has trouble enough on her
hands, poor girl!'

Presently it was reported that the patient
had fallen into a natural sleep after his long
stupor.   This was a healthy sign, and was a
great relief to all.   The doctor came to
Kate.

'I think you may venture to go in now,
and let him find you there when he wakes,'
he said.   'I shall stay here to-night to watch
the case; though I hope he will go on
favourably.'

Kate went to the sick-room.   The first
sight of Glyn was a terrible trial to her.
The results of his injuries had disfigured him
so much that she would hardly have recognised him.   She was thankful Blanche had
not come with her.

Glyn was sleeping calmly.   Kate took her
place by the bedside and watched.   By-and-by
the sufferer grew restless, and opened his

eyes. Even in the dim light Kate could see that the poor eyeballs moved about in an unmeaning manner. It was as much as she could do to control herself. The thought of her beloved brother lying there sightless was almost more than she could bear.

A faint voice came from the bed.

'Who is here ? I can't see.'

The doctor was by Kate's side. 'Speak to him now,' he whispered.

'I am here, darling Glyn,' she said, putting her hand on her brother's.

'Kate. That's well. What has happened ? Why is it I cannot see ?'

'You are very ill, Glyn. We will tell you all when you are better.'

'And you must keep absolutely quiet now,' the doctor added. 'You have had a bad accident. Quiet is the only thing for you.'

'Yes; I remember now,' Glyn said. 'The lightning; it struck me down. It has blinded me, but I trust in Heaven not for long.'

'Best let him think so,' whispered the doctor.

The patient closed his sightless eyes, and presently he slept again.

And so Kate watched in anxious silence by her brother's bedside all through the night, revolving many things in her mind. And there was one thought which, next to the hope of Glyn's recovery, was the happiest feeling at her heart—the thought of Forbes' return on the morrow. She was surprised herself at the feeling of reliance she had in his presence. It is happiness of the truest kind for a woman to lean on the man she loves— next to her trust in God, to have trust in him. That she loved Forbes she could no longer doubt, and although he had never breathed a word of love to her, she read his heart by a thousand little signs and tokens such as a woman rarely mistakes. It seemed to Kate the awakening to a heaven of happiness after long years of hopeless gloom. 'Oh, if Glyn only recovers,' she sighed, 'happiness may yet be in store for us all.'

On her knees by the bedside that night she poured forth many an earnest prayer for help and comfort, and the morning that came up sunny and bright and warm seemed to bring hope to her heart. Alas, it was soon to be dashed ! for the returning light only revealed more painfully the terrible fate which had befallen Glyn. It was dreadful to look upon his sightless orbs, and to think how keenly alive they had hitherto been to all the gladness and glory of the world — dreadful to think of the long years of darkness that might lie before him.

Quite early in the morning Glyn spoke.

'Kate, are you there ?'

'Yes, dear.'

'Come close to me ; give me your hand.'

She sat down on the bedside, letting her tears fall unrestrained.

'Kate, is she here ?'

'No, darling. She was coming with me, but poor Sib Maitland was to arrive yesterday, and Blanche could not leave her. She is very ill.'

'It is better she did not come, Kate. I could not bear it, and it would be terrible to her. She can never be anything to me now.

I am blind.   I know now—hopelessly blind.
My God!'

'Hush, Glyn!   Do not say that.   The
future is in God's hands.'

'She can never be anything to me now,
Kate.   I could not so degrade her.   Nothing
but purity should be associated with her.
Besides, how could I ask her to share the
fate of a blind man?   No, it can never be.
Promise me you will not let her come.   I
could not bear it, I tell you.   Will you
promise me?'

'If you wish it, dear.   But she will be
terribly pained, I know.'

'She may be at first, but she will learn to
know that it is for the best.   She will learn
to appreciate my motive.   Oh, my darling!
my darling!   To think that I shall never look
on that sweet face again!'

He broke into a low wail.   Kate was
terribly moved.

'Oh, Glyn, Glyn, in pity do not despair!
You do not know what may yet be in store
for you.   You may recover your sight.   The
doctor says so.'

'It is little matter one way or the other. I have been so tossed and tried lately that I am quite weary of life. I think it would have been better if the lightning had struck me dead. What hope is there for me now?'

'Glyn darling, it is your weakness makes you think this. Believe me, there are happy hours in store for you yet. If you give way to gloom like this, think how much it will keep you back. Think what she would feel if we lost you altogether.'

'Ah, there is the bitterness of it! It will be a living death to both.'

'You shall not talk like this, Glyn. You do not know how terrible it is to me to hear you. You would not wilfully pain me, I know.'

'Forgive me. I will try to be calm. But you will promise me not to send for her. I could not bear it.'

So the days passed by. The cold November days were not sadder than the hearts of the two friends as they sat by the side of their helpless invalids, the one at Lupton, the other at Firwolds. Glyn gained strength slowly, it is true; but as for Sib, they all saw that the great change might come at any moment, for fell Disease had laid upon her his relentless hand, and Sib's days were numbered.

CHAPTER LVI.

SIB HEARS THE NEWS.

'I KNOW I am keeping you here, Blanche. If it were not for me, you would be with Kate and her brother,' said Sib Maitland a few days after her arrival at Lupton.

'No, Sib, I should not. They think it is better for me not to be there at present.'

Blanche's head drooped a little as she said this. She seemed to read Glyn's motive, but there was still a mystery about it which she could not understand. They had not told her of the blindness.

'Besides, Sib, even if they wished me to come, I could not leave you.'

'That brings me to what I want to ask, Blanche. I want you to tell me the truth, dear. I know I am very ill, but at home they would not let me know all the doctor said. I know there is something kept from me. Tell me the truth, Blanche.'

'Of course you are very seriously ill, darling. It would be useless to deny that. . But there is no danger. I mean, no immediate danger.'

'But the danger may come at any moment —this is what you mean, Blanche, is it not?'

Blanche did not answer. Her heart was too full.

'You need not fear to tell me, Blanche. If I knew I was to die to-morrow I should not mind, if you will do what I ask you.'

'What is that, Sib?'

'Come nearer to me. I cannot tell you while you sit there.'

Blanche went over to the couch upon which her cousin was lying. The girl had turned her face to the window, and was looking out through the pane to the cold November day. A recent gale had stripped the trees of their verdure, and the branches

stood up weird and naked in the chill air.
Here and there an oak retained a few specks
of gold, and the deep bracken had turned to
amber amid the brown boles. Everything
denoted that saddest of all times, the dying
of the year.

Sib took her cousin's hand in her own, and
went on :

'I want you to promise me one thing,
Blanche. When it is quite sure that I am
dying—that I have not many hours to live—
you must promise me that you will send for
George. Will you promise ?'

A terrible sensation filled Blanche's heart.
She had not told Sib of D'Eyncourt's fearful
end. It was agreed on all hands that it was
better to keep it from her. What need was
there to embitter her last days—possibly to
shorten them—by the recital of a tragedy
with which she was so intimately associated ?
But now, what was she to say ? what excuse
to make ? It seemed brutal to refuse such a
request to a dying girl.

'I fancy he is abroad, Sib. I do not know
where to write to him. You know, too, how

badly he has behaved, not only to you, but
to others.'

'Blanche, Blanche! Do not say a word
against him. What is the use? No one is
without faults. I do not want to recall them,
or even to think about them. If he came
and knew, as of course he must, that I was
dying, he would be to me as he was in those
dear days when I first knew him. I want
him, if only for ten minutes, to bring back
those days. It is impossible to tell the happiness I felt then. I want to feel it once more
—to shut out all the dreadful time that has
intervened, and to let that time come back.
Oh, Blanche, you do not know the intensity
of the longing I feel to see him once more as
he was at that time! To watch his eyes as
they looked into mine, to feel his arms about
me, holding me, oh! so closely to his heart.
Blanche, you cannot refuse this when I am
dying.'

She sank her head upon her cousin's
shoulder. What was Blanche to do? It
seemed a sin to deceive a love like this, and
yet she felt that the knowledge of the truth

would kill her outright.   No ; at all hazards
it must be kept from her.   Sib went on :

'It was such a lovely time, too!   I never
remember anything like that weather.   The
sky was without a cloud all day long, and
day after day.   The flowers were so exquisite,
too—the roses in the garden and the wild-
flowers in the woods.   He used to gather
me big bunches of honeysuckle—how delicious
the perfume was !   Life was like heaven to
me then, and I looked forward to so many
years of a happy future with him.   How
strange it all seems now !'

A tear trickled and fell on Blanche's hand.
She could scarcely keep back her own, but
she had to act the part of a comforter.   She
wound her arms closely about the poor, frail
form beside her.

'I do not know why it is, Sib, but life to
most of us is one long series of disappointments.   It seems so strange in a world which
is so wondrously fair.   We do not know why
it is, but it is the lot of all.   Sib, I am not at
all sure that many of us, if they had the
choice, would not gladly change places with

you. Even if we gain our hearts' dearest desires, they often prove a source of new troubles and disappointments. There seems to be no abiding-place here. Let us hope we shall reach one by-and-by. Whatever happens, darling, you may be thankful if you are spared from the years of sorrow we most of us get in this storm-tossed world.'

' And yet there are such exquisite moments —moments of such indescribable happiness !'

' But how few and far between ! One might count such moments on one's fingers, Sib.'

' That is the bitter part of it. But, Blanche, you will try and find him, will you not ? There may not be much time to lose, darling. Sometimes now I think I have not many days to live—perhaps not many hours. There is another thing, too, I wish to say. If his life has been so wicked as you tell me it has —although I do not like to think so—it might do him good to see me. People will listen to one who is near death, and my dying words might influence all his future life. He may never even have thought of the life to

come. I did not in those days. We are
apt to forget God when we are so very, very
happy. Perhaps this is why we are so seldom
allowed to be so. You must let him come,
Blanche. You *will* try and find him at
once ?'

Absolute despair was at Blanche's heart.
What could she do ? She felt she must
temporize, even in this trying moment.

'I will do my best, Sib,' she answered.

'And at once.'

'Yes, at once.'

Sib gave a great sigh of relief.

'Oh, Blanche, you have made me so
happy !' she said. 'To see him again ! To
see him again ! Oh, thank God ! thank
God !'

She threw herself back on the couch with
upturned eyes. Her fair, delicate face seemed
transfigured. It was as if a gleam of the
glory to come had stolen through the November clouds and lighted on her brow.

Blanche could bear it no longer. She
made a hurried excuse, and hastened to her
own room. All her own pent-up anxieties

and sorrows had been stirred to their inmost depths by poor Sib's words; the long suppression had been too much, and tears came to relieve the overburthened heart.

The next fortnight was a terrible trial to Blanche. Although Sib did not recur to the subject, her cousin saw by her wistful eyes and the anxious, inquiring look that it was seldom out of her mind. She saw, too, that Sib felt her time was drawing near. At length the poor girl spoke again.

' Blanche, have you made any inquiries? she asked.

' No, darling. I did not think there was any necessity yet.'

' I think there is, Blanche. Pray do not delay. At least, try and discover where he is. Promise me this.'

It was as much as Blanche could do to keep her countenance from betraying the fatal truth. To her, whose whole life had been so truthful, this evasion was terrible, and yet she knew, if she told the truth, it would be giving Sib her death-blow. She had taken counsel of Kate, who, in a long

letter, strongly urged her not to reveal the
terrible tragedy which had taken place ; and
to have merely mentioned the fact of D'Eyncourt's death would have involved her in a
series of falsehoods, for Sib would have insisted on knowing all particulars.   She felt,
however, that it could not go on.   That poor,
worn face, for ever before her, seemed a
silent reproach which she could no longer
bear to encounter.   She resolved to take the
Vicar into her confidence, and be guided by
his advice.

'Sib, I am going to leave you for an hour
or two.   I want to go to the village.   Hooper
will stay with you, and read to you if you
wish.   It is such a lovely morning, that I
think I shall walk.'

It was indeed wonderful weather for the
time of year.   The day was one of those that
come sometimes in the early winter, but only
at rare intervals.   The air was so sunny and
bright and warm, that it seemed like the
sweet face of summer turning to look back
once more through the gloom of the winter
days.   Even the leafless branches cast off

their dull, leaden tint, and, under the scintillating sunshine, assumed a purple hue, which faded away into the soft haze of the distance in harmonious contrast to the few remaining specks of autumn gold.

'It is so lovely in the conservatory, Sib, that I think I shall leave you there. The camellias are really splendid, and there are some new ferns which will gladden your heart. I will get Hooper to arrange a comfortable couch for you.'

'Thanks. I should like it so much. How good you are to me, Blanche!'

In half an hour all was arranged. Sib was made quite comfortable on her couch, surrounded by those exquisite blooms which the floriculturist snatches from the rude hands of winter, and cherishes for our perpetual delight. The sunlight came glinting down through the delicate creepers which hung from the transparent roof above; a soft air stole in through the partly-opened glasses, and the delicate perfume of exotics pervaded the warm atmosphere. Blanche had started for the village, and Hooper, her maid, had brought some

books with which she was to amuse the sick
girl during her cousin's absence.

'It is very good of you, Hooper, but I
don't think I can listen to reading this morning. This is all so lovely, that I should like
to lie here and look about me a bit. You
need not stay. Come back in half an hour,
and see if I want anything.'

'Very well, miss. Are you sure you are
quite warm enough? Shall I get you another
shawl?'

'Oh no. It is like summer here. I shall
enjoy it so much. You may just lift this
pillow a little bit. Ah, so—that is delightful.'

'You are sure you don't want anything
more, miss?'

'Quite sure, thanks.'

She lay there very still, the only drooping
flower amid all the lovely blooms around.
All was so sunny and calm, that by-and-by a
pleasant drowsiness stole over her and she
closed her eyes. Sib's nights were sorely
troubled now. The racking cough, which
worries the consumptive patient to the last,
kept her awake for hours, so that when

Hooper returned at the appointed time, and found her, as she thought, sleeping, she rejoiced greatly, and stole away again on tip-toe.

But Sib was not asleep. Her thoughts had gone back to that time which was never absent from her mind—to the days of early love, to the summer woods and the moonlit terrace, and the thousand vivid remembrances of the time when life had been like a foretaste of heaven. It all came back to her with wonderful vividness to-day. The faint perfume around her, and the warm air, were positively suggestive of those summer days. Where was D'Eyncourt now, she wondered ? Had he entirely forgotten her, or was there still a lingering trace of the love which he had professed in tones which went to her very heart ? Doubtless he had gone through many trials. If life had been all smooth to him, he might have been true to her. She fancied he would have been, for she could not even now bring herself to believe in such wilful wickedness as the reverse involved. It was little matter now, however. There was no power on earth, she knew, that could snatch her from the fatal grasp that death had laid upon her.   But she must see him before she died.   Blanche had promised this, and this was her only hope or desire in life now.

By-and-by she passed from waking remembrances to the memories that come back to us in sleep.   Her head sank back upon the pillow, her hand dropped by her side, she glided into what seemed complete oblivion. Oblivion!   No.   With that strange incongruity which must always remain a mystery to psychologists, remembrance became more vivid when slumber fell upon the brain.   She not only remembered ; she lived and moved in that delightful time of early love.   D'Eyncourt was by her side—she felt the warm pressure of his hand, she heard his fervent words.   She absolutely saw the fatal beauty of his face.   He wound his arms about her, and again a delirious joy stole into her heart as his lips met hers.   The feeling was too intense.   With a low cry of exquisite happiness, she awoke.

The sounds of real voices were coming in through the half-opened glasses of the conser-

vatory — voices of two gardeners who had
paused in their work, and who were utterly
oblivious of the proximity of anyone who
could overhear them. The air was so still
that every word fell upon Sib's ear with
peculiar distinctness.

' I'll never believe Captain D'Eyncourt did
it. He's a wild one, I know—a regular dare-
devil—but he wouldn't commit a murder in
cold blood. He's too much of a gentleman.'

' But look at the facts, Tom. Look at the
facts.'

' Facts be blowed! Anyone else might
have knocked young Mr. Beverley on the
head besides the Captain. I don't believe
he did it.'

' That's all very well, but go into it bit by
bit. What can you say then ? Here, now.
It's known that Mr. Beverley was with the
Captain in the afternoon. Nobody knows
what passed between 'em, but he was there.
Well, he goes away to walk to the station
just afore the storm began. Two minutes
after the Captain comes out and tells the

groom to saddle the fastest mare in the stable.
Then away he goes, as he says, to Brighton.
Well, half an hour after Mr. Beverley is
picked up with a cracked skull in the road
leading to the station, and not far off in a
field are found the marks of a horse's hoofs
which correspond exactly with the feet of the
mare the Captain rode.   Then, next day,
what do they find at the bottom of a chalk-
pit, quite away from the Brighton road, but
the dead body of the Captain, and his horse
dead beside him ; and in the breast-pocket of
his coat is a weapon covered with blood
which—— Good Lord ! what's that ?'
     A long, low, terrible moan which seemed
to come from a breaking heart.   The man
stopped, horror-stricken.   Then he looked at
his companion, then stole noiselessly towards
the conservatory.   Through the thick leaves
and the camellia blooms he saw the drapery
of a woman stretched supine upon a couch.
     He could not see the face.   If he had
looked upon it, he would have looked upon
the face of death.
     His words—his fatal words—had snapped

the feeble cord, and Sib's soul had gone upward—

'To where beyond these voices there is peace.'

Will the whiteness of her soul be deemed a sufficient atonement for the blackness of his whom she loved so well, when the two shall stand face to face upon the Awful Threshold?

CHAPTER LVII.

GLYN'S RESOLVE.

FORBES was almost established at Firwolds now. As Glyn gained strength, which he did rapidly, his friend became more and more useful in a thousand ways. He had taken up his abode at a hotel near the station, so that he was always near at hand, and generally spent the whole day at Firwolds.

There was no difficulty now about the property. D'Eyncourt's death had removed every obstacle. Mr. Norwood was hard at work not only in getting this settled, but in establishing the illegality of Glyn's unlucky marriage.

Forbes usually arrived early and found Kate in the breakfast-room. On one

occasion she was not there. He inquired
of the servant where she was.

'Miss Beverley has had some very bad
news this morning, sir; she told me to let
her know when you arrived.'

Forbes vainly endeavoured to conjecture
what this new calamity could be. He was
not kept long waiting. Kate came down as
soon as she heard of his arrival, her eyes
wet with tears.

'Oh, Mr. Forbes! There is such terrible
news. Poor Sib is dead.'

'Dead?' echoed Forbes.

'Yes; and so suddenly. Blanche is over-
whelmed with grief. She left her for a few
hours while she went to the village. On her
way back she met Hooper with the carriage.
She was hastening down to tell her poor Sib
was gone.'

'How very dreadful!'

'It is too terrible, said Kate, her tears
breaking out afresh. 'I am in such a difficulty, too,' she went on. 'I must go to
Blanche, and I do not like leaving Glyn.
What is to be done?'

'Pray don't take it so to heart, Miss Beverley,' said Forbes. 'Let me stay with Glyn. He does not actually need you now, and I shall be so very glad to help you in the difficulty, don't you know.'

'How good you are! I don't know what I should have done all this dreadful time without your help.'

Kate was sitting on a couch near the window, her eyes still wet with tears. Forbes suddenly seated himself by her side and placed his hand on hers.

'Look here, Kate,' he said, calling her for the first time by her Christian name : 'I don't know whether I am going to make an awful fool of myself, and I fear this is hardly the time to speak, but I must take the chance. I love you better than anything in the world, and I want you to be my wife. Then I shall have the right to help you in every way, you know.'

Kate trembled all over, and her cheeks turned to the colour of roses ; but she did not take away the hand which Forbes now held in a close clasp.

'Oh, Mr. Forbes; I am not worthy of you,' she said.

It was not affectation, for she looked upon Forbes as the best man in the world, and she loved him with her whole heart and soul.

'Don't say that, Kate. I know that it is very much the other way. I am a heavy, stupid sort of fellow, not fit to hold a candle to your brother; but you will never find one who loves you more truly. Will you take me as I am? Only say yes, and I shall be the happiest fellow in the world.'

Kate took him at his word. Looking up to him with still streaming eyes, she answered simply 'Yes,' and then——

But there is no need to particularize what followed. We know the usual result of a compact like this, when the compact springs from the impulse of two loving hearts.

'So now,' said Forbes, 'you can go without any compunctions with regard to your brother. He will be my brother as well in future. You may depend I shall take good care of him while you are away.'

'I shall feel perfectly happy about him.'

'But I say, Kate, I can't wait long without seeing you again. If you are not back in a few days, I must run over and see you at Lupton.'

'I shall so long for the time to come,' said ingenuous Kate. 'I have learned to rely on you so much that I don't know how I could face the future without you. But we must wait until these few sad days are over. Poor darling Sib! what a troubled life she has had!'

Glyn received the news of what had passed between Kate and Forbes with great rejoicing. He felt quite contented with the arrangement which left him in the charge of the latter. Indeed, he was most anxious that his sister should be with Blanche now that this new sorrow had descended on her. There seemed to be no end to the complications of grief. He was getting more and more confirmed in the belief that it was useless to look for anything but a succession of troubles in this life.

And, indeed, it was no wonder in this case.

The remembrance of all he had gone through, the thought that his eyes were darkened, perhaps for ever, to the light and beauty of the world, that his blindness, whatever might happen, was an effectual barrier between himself and the woman he loved—all this pressed . upon him until he became absolutely morbid. The darkest thoughts filled his mind when he thought of his future.

'It would have been better if the lightning had finished me altogether, Forbes,' he said one day after Kate had taken her departure for Lupton. 'Think what a wretched existence I shall have to drag out for the remainder of my days! Think of having to live, perhaps fifty years, in darkness, without love and without hope.'

'Not without love, old man; you have your sister. There cannot be a more loving heart than hers.'

Forbes purposely avoided any reference to Blanche; he knew that in Glyn's present state of mind it was delicate ground.

'But you will take her from me,' said Glyn. 'I don't complain, God knows. It will be a happy future for her, poor girl! still, it must make my life more lonely.'

'I will do nothing of the kind. You cannot suppose I should be such an awful brute as to take her from you. No, we will live together, and you will have two nurses instead of one, don't you know.'

'That's all very well. I know your intentions are good, but it would be an impossibility. She would have all sorts of things to attend to. She would wish to devote her whole time and thoughts to you and your comforts. It is but natural. I could not expect her to go on attending to my whims and fancies after she is married.'

'You take a morbid view of the case, Glyn. It would be our greatest pleasure to attend to your wants and comforts.'

'You think so now, and it is very good of you, but I could not be a burthen on anyone. No, no! When you are married, I must do the best I can for myself. Nobody but a wife could attend to a poor broken-down wretch in such a condition as mine, and I could not now ask any woman to marry me.'

With a sudden impulse, Forbes ventured on what he knew was forbidden ground.

'I know a woman who would marry you,' he said. 'The best woman in all this world, bar one.'

Glyn uttered an angry exclamation.

'I have said over and over again I would not have that referred to. It is absolute torture to me. Good Heaven! do you think I could ask her to share a lot like mine? She, so full of youth, and health, and beauty, surrounded by wealth and luxury, to become the constant nurse of a poor blind creature like myself! Besides, you know what I feel about that other woman. I have lived with her as her husband. However illegal the marriage may have been, it has left a taint on me. I could never ask Blanche to be my wife—at least, not while that woman lives.'

'This is quixotic,' said Forbes.

'It is not. It is but justice to a pure woman. Even supposing, for the sake of argument, that she could bring herself to accept me as I am, think what my feeling would be. I should be haunted perpetually

by the thought of the fate to which I had
doomed her. You must remember what the
future may be. When the recollection of all
this recent sorrow has passed, as it is but
natural it will, she will take her place in the
world. You must remember that her social
station is a high one. Her gentle heart and
simple tastes have led her to relinquish it to
some extent. It is one of my bitterest
thoughts that possibly I may have been the
cause. She will return to that station in
time. She will be courted and admired
wherever she goes. She might marry
among the highest in the land. Can I drag
her down from such a prospect as this ? But
yet the reverse is too terrible, and I have
loved her so dearly.'

He broke down altogether. Forbes went
over and laid his hand upon his shoulder.

'Come, come, old man, this will never do ,
you will think differently about these things
when you are better.'

'Ah! that is just the one thing I dread
—the thought that I may give way. I have
pondered over this matter for hours and

hours, Forbes. I am wondering whether you will help me in something I want to do.'

'What is it?'

'Simply, as soon as I am strong enough, to go away from this abroad somewhere—to the South of France or Italy. Of course I can't do so alone, and I can't take Kate away from her friend at present.'

'But why should you do this? There is not the least necessity for it.'

'There is the strongest necessity for it. As long as I am here her sympathies will be constantly on the alert. Sooner or later, I believe she would come to me. This is what I want to avoid, for it must not be. Do you hear? It *must* not! If I am away, if there is no possibility of our being thrown together, she would in time turn to other thoughts and pursuits. It is only natural that she should. She might even forget me altogether. It is the only chance for me, too. Here I am perpetually on the rack— not only with intense longing to see her, but from the fear that she may come. If I could carry out the plan I propose, it would be best for both of us in the end. In any case, it is but justice to her, and would give her the chance of a brighter future than she could ever have with me—God help me!'

Forbes could not but admit that there was much truth in what Glyn said. He admired the single-heartedness which prompted his poor friend to accept banishment rather than permit a sacrifice on the part of the woman he loved. He did not, however, see his way.

'Kate would never consent to your going alone, Glyn,' he said.

'She would if you were with me. I do not ask you to stay. Only see me safely settled. I can afford to pay for careful nursing now. I can obtain all the attention I want with money. It is not a pleasant alternative, but I should feel more independent. Gold must take the place of love in future.'

He gave a bitter laugh, which was inexpressibly painful to Forbes. It seemed to indicate so completely the wreck of the genial temperament he had known so recently.

'If I go with you, I go to stay,' he answered. 'There will be no half-measures with me.'

'That I cannot consent to,' said Glyn. 'I might have done so a week ago, but now things are altered. There is Kate to be considered. No; you shall take me there and leave me there, and the sooner it is done the better.'

'But you are not fit to travel yet.'

'I shall be in a week or two. Between ourselves, I have spoken to the doctor about it. He says, in my shattered state, a winter in the South of France would be the very best thing for me.'

Forbes was sorely puzzled. He felt there was sense in what Glyn proposed. At any rate, the separation would be a test of affection, under these most distressing circumstances. He could not, however, make up his mind to consent at once. Besides, there was another to be consulted now in all things which pertained to himself. He therefore begged Glyn to give him a few days to think over his proposition.

Then, as soon as the funeral of poor Sib was over, he wrote a long letter to Kate, telling her all that had passed.

And Kate read the letter to Blanche as they sat together the following morning. To her surprise, Blanche did not say a word for several minutes, but a look of quiet resolution was in her face. At length Kate asked her what she thought.

'I think it will be better to let him have his own way. I see all that is in his thoughts, and it only makes me love him the more. Perhaps by-and-by, when he has had time to think over these things, he may come to a different conclusion—especially if he finds that I can never change.'

And then a tear trickled down Blanche's cheek, and Kate came over to her and put her arms about her, and the two girls wept in unison, and felt they were bound together by stronger ties than ever.

CHAPTER LVIII.

FORBES GROWS ANXIOUS.

EIGHT months had passed away. The time of primroses had come again. They were bright over all the woods of Lupton, which were a perfect paradise of early flowers.

Kate Beverley was sitting at a small writing-table in the recess of a window in the morning-room. A pen was in her hand, but she was not writing. Her thoughts were far away, her eyes wandering over the beauty of garden, park, and hilly distance ; her ears taking in, unconsciously, the mellow murmur of the bees, the twittering of the birds, and the far-off echo of the cuckoo 'telling his name to all the hills' from the wood below.

She had paused in the midst of a letter to

Forbes—about the fiftieth she had written in the last eight months—for her lover would not rest without one or two a week. She was growing restless and unhappy at the prolonged wandering of the two friends ; for Glyn would not return, and Forbes would not leave him. Indeed, he knew that, in spite of the pain of separation, he was pleasing Kate by remaining.

Glyn's condition caused him the greatest anxiety. Whether it was from the injuries he had received, or from the mental torture he had undergone, Forbes could not tell, but he was falling deeper and deeper into a state of morbid gloom from which no efforts of his friend could arouse him. It was a time of real trial to Forbes, a trial that was aggravated by his having no one to share his troubles. Out of consideration to Kate he had to a great extent concealed Glyn's depression from her. He went on hoping from day to day that a change for the better might come, and he therefore wrote as cheerfully as he possibly could respecting her brother.

Glyn took the strangest fancies. Blind as

he was, he insisted on travelling to Rome
and Naples.   It was the saddest sight possible
to see him in the midst of the wonders of the
Eternal City, or on the shores of the exquisite
Bay of Naples, insisting on the minutest de-
scription of every object or scene that was
before them.

'Place me now facing Vesuvius,' he would
say, when they were on the sea-shore at
Naples.   'I feel the soft air from off the sea.
I hear the lapping of the waves, the prattle
of the children's voices.   Tell me the colour
of the sea, the shape of the boats, the tint of
the distant mountains, and I shall see it all in
my mind's eye.

Or at Rome in the sculpture-galleries he
would make Forbes lead him from one
masterly group to another, and touch them
with his hand, and gaze towards them with
his sightless orbs until his constant friend
was quite overcome by the earnest longing
in the sad face, and felt that he would have
almost sacrificed his own sight to have given
Glyn a glimpse of those wonders, to see
which had been the one great longing of his

life.   But this could not go on, for reaction
followed the temporary excitement which
Glyn felt at being actually amid these
wondrous scenes.   After a time their
presence only increased the depression
caused by his terrible deprivation.

'What am I to do?' he would cry.
'Where go?   How can I find relief?   Why
are health and strength again given to me, if
beauty and sunshine are for ever shut out?
Even my wealth comes as a mockery now.
If I had but died that night when the lightning struck me, how much better it would
have been!'

This was the sort of thing Forbes had to
listen to day after day.   He would have
endured it, if only to satisfy the promptings
of his kind heart; but when he felt besides
that it was for the sake of Kate's brother, he
bore it all cheerfully, and always had a word
of encouragement and hope.   But Kate did
not know all this; she was to learn it afterwards from Glyn's own lips.   She knew that
her brother was restless and unhappy, and insisted on moving from place to place.   She

felt that this was quite a sufficient trial to so warm a heart as her lover's, and she was on this particular morning pausing to think how best she could repay him for all his loving self-sacrifice.

Suddenly, in the midst of her musings, she heard a step in the hall; the door of the room opened; she turned, and the next moment Forbes himself was in the room.

She started up and ran forward with a little cry. Then her lover's strong arms were folded about her, holding her in a close embrace.

'My darling, do I really see you once more after all this time?' he said.

She could scarcely speak for happiness, scarcely keep down the sobs that came from intensity of joy.

'I was just writing to you,' she said. 'Oh, how little I thought you were so near! How good you have been! What can I ever do to repay you?'

'We will talk of that by-and-by, darling. I dare say you will find a way.'

'But what of Glyn? Is he back, too?'

'Yes. We both returned only yesterday
—quite suddenly.'

'But what has brought you back? You
said in your last you could not persuade him
to come.'

'I think the immediate cause was a letter.
He won't confess it, but when I suggested
coming, as I had done a thousand times
before, he offered no opposition.'

'What letter?'

'I have brought it to show you. But you
are trembling still, darling. Sit here, and I
will read it to you. By the way, where is
your friend Blanche? she ought to hear it,
too.'

'I think she is gone to the village. She
is very busy about her schools and various
matters. Very good in every way, you may
be sure.'

'Is she still silent on the subject of Glyn,
as you told me she was in your letters?'

'Yes, she seldom refers to him. I think
she felt his going more deeply than ever I
imagined. I can understand and respect her
silence. It is a very, very difficult position.

Even now I cannot say that Glyn was wholly wrong. Good as she is, it would have been a terrible fate to be bound for life to a blind man. But about this letter?'

'It is here—stay, you had better read it yourself.'

Forbes placed the letter in Kate's hand, and watched her face as she read. It was as follows :

'Philadelphia,
'May 16, 187—.

'My dear Glyn,

'I think it may be a relief to you to hear that I am going to be married again very shortly. I have met with a gentleman, Count D'Epigny, who seems in every way suited to me, and who, I am sure, will make me happy. He is very amiable and ac-complished, but with narrow means. Of course this last does not matter, as I have plenty for both. I thought it right to give you the earliest information, as you need have no further anxiety about me. We shall remain here for some time, as the Count is engaged in some engineering works. When they are completed, we shall probably reside in Italy, or somewhere on the Continent. I like America pretty well. The people are, on the whole, very nice—the men very attentive. I have had very little news from England. I trust you are well and happy. I should like to hear of you sometimes.

'I read the announcement of *his* death in the papers, but have had no particulars. You may imagine what I felt. With best love,

'Ever yours affectionately,

'LAURA.'

Kate put down the letter in silent astonishment.

'What do you think of it?' asked Forbes.

'I think she is the most amazing woman I ever heard of,' said Kate.

'She has the knack of taking life easily, any way,' said Forbes.

'Of course Glyn will have nothing more to do with her,' Kate went on. 'What did he say when he heard the letter?'

'He only laughed. It was rather a bitter

laugh, I must admit, but I am glad he took it in that way.'

'After all, I forgive her for this. It is about the best thing that could happen for poor dear Glyn. But what a wretched thing for the poor man!'

'If he is not an adventurer, which I think highly probable,' said Forbes.

'It will serve her right if he is. But do not let us talk about it. I feel furious with indignation when I think of that woman, and I am too happy this morning to feel furious with anyone. Tell me about Glyn. Is there any improvement in him yet?'

Forbes hesitated a moment before he answered; then he said:

'Kate darling, I fear I must prepare you for very bad news about him. I have not told you all in my letters. It was useless distressing you, as you could do no good.'

'Oh, what is it?' Kate cried, looking at him with eager eyes. 'Is he seriously ill?'

'It is not his bodily ailments to which I refer, Kate. It is his mind. He suffers from such intense fits of depression, that at times I am seriously alarmed. I sometimes feel afraid he may lose his reason.'

'Oh, no, no!' cried Kate; 'this is too dreadful. I must go to him at once.'

'My darling, I do not see that your going would do him any good—at least, only temporarily. He sits for hours without speaking. No efforts of mine will rouse him. And, unfortunately, the fits are becoming worse.'

'What can be done? Poor darling Glyn! Oh, how much he has suffered!'

'There is only one thing that would do him good—one person, I should say—that is Blanche. And he would never consent to meet her, I fear. Indeed, we do not now know what her feelings may be.'

'I think I can answer for her. I believe she loves him more dearly than ever, although she says nothing.'

'Shall we tell her?'

'I think so. She has such good sense that she may suggest something. At any rate, we must tell her. It would be unfair to keep it from her.'

Presently Blanche returned, and, after she had somewhat recovered from the surprise and evident emotion caused by Forbes' sudden appearance, they told her of Glyn's condition, and showed her the letter from Laura.

She turned very pale, but for a few minutes she did not speak. Presently she said :

'Of course you will go to him at once, Kate.'

'Yes, that is my intention,' Kate answered.

'You must let me go with you, but you must promise not to reveal my presence in the house until I see a favourable opportunity of making it known. Will you consent to this ?'

'We shall be only too glad to leave every-thing to you,' said Forbes. 'I can assure you of one thing, Miss Venables : If your presence does not rouse him, I dread to think of the future. It is impossible to say what this morbid gloom may end in.'

CHAPTER LIX.

ON THE TERRACE.

On the way to Firwolds, Forbes gave a more detailed account of his wanderings with Glyn abroad. Blanche listened with intense eagerness, but said very little. As for poor Kate, her tears flowed afresh as every new incident was narrated.

The anxious time he had gone through had quite altered Forbes. It was the first break in the smooth monotony of his life. There were actual lines of care in his face, formerly so round and rubicund. Kate had noticed this at the first glance, and she felt that, to a great extent, it was for her that her lover had voluntarily endured this time of trial. As they neared Firwolds, Blanche spoke on the subject again.

' I have another request to make,' she said.
' If he should inquire about me, I want you
to lead him to suppose that I am fairly well
and happy. He may ask what I said about
him. You can say, and say truly, that I have
said very little. I have a strong motive for
making this request, and I know you will
grant it.'

They both seemed to read her thoughts,
and, of course, consented.

' You will give me every facility also for
watching him without his knowing I am there.
It will not last for long. In a day, or at the
most two, I shall have made up my mind
whether or not to make my presence known.'

There was a strange calmness about
Blanche as she gave these directions.
Although to some extent they saw her
motive, it was next to impossible to detect
the real feelings of her heart. Kate had even
doubted once or twice whether she really did
care for Glyn as much as she used to do.

' I had forgotten to tell you that we saw
the doctor again as we came through
London,' said Forbes. ' He made another

careful examination of the eyes. He thinks, after all, that the blindness was due to the lightning, as Glyn said.'

'Did he give any hope?'

'Yes. He said he thought he detected some improvement. The worst feature was the length of time he had remained blind. Of course, as he said, these cases are very rare, but people who are struck blind by lightning usually recover their sight much sooner. Unfortunately this dreadful depression tends to retard his recovery. It seems that the lightning paralyzes the optic nerve. Anything, therefore, that depresses the nervous system diminishes the chances of recovery.'

'Therefore health and cheerfulness would facilitate his recovery,' said Blanche quickly.

'Exactly. If this terrible depression could be shaken off, his chances of recovery would be infinitely greater.'

'Did the doctor tell him this?' asked Kate.

'Yes; but it had little effect. It is useless hiding the truth, but, really, I think he has

sunk into such a morbid state that he does
not care to recover. You will see for your-
selves.'

On reaching Firwolds, Forbes went at
once to find Glyn and to prepare him for
Kate's arrival. He was in none of the lower
rooms. On inquiring of the servant, the
man informed him that Mr. Beverley was
walking on the terrace in front of the house.

' This is what he has done in almost every
place we have visited,' Forbes said. ' He
has some space measured out near a wall or
balustrade ; then he paces it himself, and
afterwards walks up and down for hours ; I
believe, without counting, he knows exactly
when he is at the end of so many paces.
He then turns and walks back again,
occasionally feeling the wall, or whatever it
may be, with his stick. I let him have his
way, for he hates to be dependent even on
my arm.'

They proceeded to the drawing-room, the
low windows of which opened to the terrace.
Blanche still preserved the strange calmness
which she had maintained all the morning,

but Kate was so overcome at the thought of again meeting her brother under such painful conditions that she could hardly stand.   They went to one of the windows and stood there while Forbes passed out on to the terrace and advanced towards Glyn.

At the sound of his footstep on the gravel Glyn stopped and turned.

In spite of her forced calmness, Blanche could hardly suppress a cry.

She had not seen Glyn since the day they had visited Sutton-Colville together.   He had passed through the Valley of the Shadow of Death since that time.   The face was so wan and worn, so full of the traces of acute suffering—both mental and bodily—that she would hardly have recognised him.   His form, too, had shrunk to half its former dimensions, and, saddest sight of all, the eyes which once looked into her own, full of the light of love, were now dark and meaningless, and, though turned towards her, were utterly unconscious of her presence.

She sank into a chair in the recess of the window.   All the colour had died out of her face.   She sat with clasped hands, the very picture of despair.

'Oh, Kate, Kate, this is too dreadful!' she whispered.   'What tortures he must have endured to reduce him to that!'

'Hush, darling; do not let him hear you,' said Kate, who was herself trembling in every limb.   'I am so anxious to see what he will do.'

With a great effort Blanche controlled her emotion, and stood beside Kate, watching.

When Forbes was within two or three yards of him, Glyn spoke:

'Is that you, Forbes?'

'Yes.   I have got back all right.'

'Is Kate come?'

'Yes.'

'Where is she?'

Forbes made a sign for her to advance. She went forward quickly. Glyn's face betrayed but little emotion.

'I knew your step, Kate,' he said.   'You must come and kiss me, for I can't come to kiss you.'

The next moment his sister's arms were

round his neck, and her lips pressed to his pale cheek.

She dared not trust herself to speak for fear of breaking down utterly.

In spite of his blindness, Glyn was conscious of the struggle she was undergoing.   He put her from him almost abruptly.

'Don't let us have any tears, Kate ; I can't stand it.   We have had enough of senti-ment and emotion.   It is better to steel one's heart.'

Kate drew herself from him with a new pang at her breast.   Then she passed her hand gently within his arm.

'I don't want help, Kate.   I have learned to be self-reliant.   Here is my beat.   I walk up and down here by the hour, like a wild beast in a cage.'

'Oh, Glyn, do not talk in that way !' Kate cried.

'Why not ?' he said bitterly.   'In what is my condition better ?   What can be a more effectual cage than this blindness ?   One might as well be in a dungeon as in this eternal darkness.'

He was silent for a few moments.   Then
he suddenly resumed his walk, with Kate
pacing by his side.   Presently he stopped
again.

'How is Blanche?' he asked abruptly.

Kate remembered her instructions, though
it cost her an effort to carry them out.

'She is very well, Glyn.   Very busy, as
usual.'

'And happy?'

'Yes ; I hope so.   She has a great deal on
her hands, as you may imagine.'

'Plenty to occupy her thoughts.   Ah!'
Another pause.   Then another rapid question:
'Forbes, are you there?'

'Yes.'

'Did you see Blanche?'

'Yes.'

'Tell me how she was looking.   You
could best judge, as you have not seen her
for so long.'

'She was looking fairly well.'

'Very well?'

'Yes ; very well.'

Another turn on the terrace, and then :

'Did she ask for me?'

'Naturally she did.'

'And I hope you said I was very well. You did not give a bad account of me, I trust.'

'I told her what the doctor said of you.'

'That there was very little hope?'

'He hardly said that. He told me if you could shake off this despondency you might yet recover your sight.'

'He said that, did he? Did he tell you how I was to shake it off? Did he give you some medicine for a mind diseased?'

'Come, come, Glyn! You know I never answer you when you talk like that.'

'No; you leave me to get out of my fit as I best can. Well, perhaps you are right. This is the way we go on, you see, Kate. He knows me well, I promise you.'

Another pause. Blanche had stolen from the window, and was within a few yards of where they were walking. She made a sign of caution to Kate. She did not yet wish her presence known. Glyn stopped again.

'You see, I was right,' he said, striking

his stick upon the ground. 'You must both admit I was right. I tore myself away from her when I believe if I had made a sign she would have come. I knew that if she had time to think calmly she would come to a different mind—that she would see the folly, the madness, of linking her fate with a broken-down wretch like me. I won't say what it has cost me to do this, but you see now—in fact, you yourself tell me that she is well and happy. Therefore you see I was right.' A few more rapid steps, and then : 'You must never let her come here now. It is I who must be considered in future. She has regained her peace of mind. Mine is yet to come. And, look here,' he added almost fiercely, 'you must never sympathize with me, never attempt to utter one word of consolation. I want my heart to turn to stone —to stone, I tell you ! There must be no thought of feeling, of tender emotions, never any more. Never let me hear another word of sympathy until all feelings are dead— dead.'

He went on his way quickly in his blindness and misery. Unutterably shocked, Kate could only stand there weeping.

But a great light came into Blanche's face, a light like the radiance one dreams of in the faces of angels. Still she made no sign, except of caution.

'Now, you two happy lovers, go and take a walk,' said Glyn. 'Leave me here to take my walk alone. I shall get on very well; and, mind, you are not to fret about me, for I won't have it. Be off, both of you.'

They left him without a word, Blanche following them. When they were out of hearing they stopped.

'What are we to do?' asked Forbes.

'Do what he asks you,' answered Blanche. ' Leave me here to watch him. Only caution the servants not to let him know I am here at all.'

They saw she really wished it, and they went. It had been almost more than Kate could bear. They went their way across the grass, while Blanche returned to the angle of the terrace and watched unperceived.

CHAPTER LX.

RESCUE.

GLYN stood listening eagerly until the footsteps had died away. Then he turned suddenly towards the stone balustrade of the terrace, and, stretching his arms over it, looked upward, as if in prayer.

Blanche could see his lips moving, but no sound was audible. There was a look of utter desolation in his face. She could bear it no longer. She was about to advance, when Glyn turned suddenly, and began moving slowly towards the house.

What would he say if she made her presence known ? Might he not still be obdurate ? Might it not cause him to undergo another struggle, even worse than those he had already

endured ? She wanted to read his heart completely before she ran the risk.

Feeling with his stick before him, he
reached the open window, and passed slowly
into the house. Blanche stepped on to the
turf which bordered the broad gravel walk,
and advanced quickly to a point from which
she could see into the room.

Glyn passed across the room towards the
fireplace and rang the bell. Then he sat
down in an easy-chair.

The servant appeared in answer to the bell.

' Is that Parker ?' asked Glyn.

' Yes, sir.'

' Parker, I have this troublesome earache
again. They say laudanum is a good thing.
Do you know if there is any in the house ?'

' I don't know, sir, but I'll inquire.'

The servant departed. Glyn sat quite
still in the same attitude. Blanche stood
behind a shrub close by the open window, so
that she could hear distinctly all that was
said in the room.

Parker returned with a small bottle in his
hand.

'Mrs. Wyatt had some, sir. What shall I do with it?'

'Do you think you could manage to pour a few drops in my ear?'

'I dare say I can, sir.'

'Stay, I just want to do some writing first; then I'll get you to do it, and sit quiet after it for a bit. Leave it on the mantelpiece.'

'Yes, sir. I needn't say you must be careful with it, sir.'

'Oh, nobody will touch it there; besides, a small quantity would do no harm.'

'I beg your pardon, sir; there's enough to kill two people in that bottle.'

'Well, it will only be for two or three minutes, and no one is likely to come here in that time.'

'Very well, sir.'

The door closed, and Glyn was left alone. For a long time there was no sound. Blanche was afraid to move, almost to breathe, for fear of betraying her presence. Presently there was a long-drawn sigh, and then she heard Glyn rise and his footsteps approaching. He came towards the window again,

and she could see him now quite plainly.
What would he do during the absence of
Forbes and Kate ?   How would he employ
himself?   If she could watch him for an
hour or so, it would be some indication to
her of what his life was, what his future
would be.   She wished to read his very
thoughts.

He came close to a table on which were
writing materials.   He sat down at it, and,
with the facility of touch acquired by blind
people, he found pen, ink, and paper.   Stretching the paper before him, he began writing,
previously passing his finger over the surface
to ascertain if it was a blank sheet.

He paused a moment, raising his sightless
eyes to the light outside the window.   He
appeared in deep thought.   Then he stooped
over the paper, and, feeling for the right
place on the sheet with the finger of his left
hand, began writing.

He wrote for several minutes — slowly,
laboriously, as if with extreme care.   A
slight movement of the finger indicated each
new line ; the practised hand of the artist

kept the lines straight, although invisible to
him.

Presently he stopped. Blanche could see
that the characters on the paper were traced
with marvellous precision for one in Glyn's
condition. She had a burning longing to see
what he had written. Vague forebodings
filled her breast, which she had hardly yet
realized to herself.

Suddenly Glyn rose. He felt his way
towards the window, leaving the unfolded
sheet upon the table. He passed through
the open window. By raising her hand
Blanche could have touched him, but still,
by an effort, she restrained herself.

Within a yard of her Glyn stopped. Did
some consciousness of her presence cross his
mind? He turned his eyes full upon her.
Oh, the sorrow of that look! It never faded
from her mind.

She held her breath. The rustle of a
garment, the movement of a finger, might
have betrayed her. But there was no
breeze. The sunshine lay warm and still
upon the ground, and Glyn moved on, and

once more leaned over the balustrade of the terrace.

Then, without an instant's hesitation, she passed noiselessly through the window, and read what lay upon the table. This was what she saw:

' My Darling,

'I can no longer endure existence apart from you. I have accomplished the end for which I lived. They tell me you are well and fairly happy; God in heaven grant that you may always remain so. Forgive my rash act, and believe that your dear name is the last sound that my lips will utter. May God for ever bless you!

'Glyn.'

Her forebodings were realized now. She saw it all with a sickening of heart which almost caused her to drop. The necessity— the dire necessity for instant action was before her. There was no retreating now, even if she had wished to, for Glyn's return- ing form darkened the window. As quick as thought, she glided over to the mantel-piece.

The bottle of laudanum was still there, nearly full, as Parker had left it.

The sight restored her, and a desperate calmness succeeded to the anguish of the previous moment.   In an instant she had stationed herself close beside where it stood.

Glyn was feeling his way towards the writing-table.   He placed his hand upon the sheet of paper, folded it, found an envelope in a case hard by, and, placing the paper within it, sat down and addressed it with a firm hand.

'God for ever bless her and forgive me my sin!' he said aloud.

Then he placed the letter on the table, and came towards the mantelpiece.

He passed his hand carefully along the shelf, feeling for the bottle.   There was no mistaking his deadly purpose.   With white face and quivering lips he laid his fingers on the fatal phial.   With his left hand he withdrew the cork, and the next moment was raising the bottle to his lips.

There was a low, hysterical cry close beside him, and the bottle was torn from his grasp. Then soft arms were wound about him, and a well-remembered voice sounded in his ear :

'Oh, Glyn, Glyn! my love! my darling! Would you tear yourself from me for ever?'

With a cry of actual terror, Glyn sank backward into a chair.

'Blanche!' he cried, with white and conscience-stricken face. 'Why are you here?'

'To save you from yourself, Glyn—by the mercy of Heaven to save you from this fearful act. Oh, thank God that I was in time!'

Closer and closer she wound her arms about him, and drew his face to hers, and kissed his brow and cheeks and sightless eyes. There was no mistaking the intensity of her embraces—no mistaking the depth of the love that prompted them.

'This is heaven!' murmured Glyn, as he threw his own arms about her, holding her closer and closer to his heart. 'My darling, do you mean to tell me you love me still?'

'Love you! Oh, Glyn, dear as you were to me in the old days, my love was weak compared with what I feel for you in your affliction. Oh, Glyn, Glyn, why did you not trust me, and believe that I was yours for ever? My darling, let me kiss away the tears from those poor eyes! Let me feel that I shall never, never leave you again, but be yours to help and guide you through your lonely, darkened life. Let me be light and sunshine to you, Glyn, for I have no other hope or wish in this world.'

And a wondrous peace fell upon Glyn's heart, and through the darkness and the trouble came the gleam of a great hope.

Once more the summer sunshine is bright over all the woods of Lupton. The cuckoo, with its namesake the flower, has departed; the woodbine is scenting the summer air, and the foxglove raises its dappled spires in every leafy glade.

In the self-same spot where Glyn had set
up his easel two summers before, he is again
at work, gazing with unclouded eyes over the
blue distance, which, seen between the stems
of the beeches, melts away into infinite space.
He is alone, but near at hand is the sound of
an unseen companion, moving within the
encircling foliage.

He pauses for a noonday rest, and puts
down his palette.

'Blanche!' he calls softly.

'Yes, dear,' is the answer from behind the
branches.

'Come here; I can't bear you out of my
sight for a moment, wife.'

Blanche comes from amidst the foliage,
laden with wild-flowers, and mosses, and
trailing ivy.

'I know you will like these for your study,
dear,' she says. 'Does the work try your
eyes?'

'Not in the least; but I shall rest them
now, and I must have you near me.'

She comes and sits on the ground by his
side, leaning her head upon his knee. He

passes his hand down her soft brown hair until it lights lovingly on her neck.

'Was I not right?' she says. 'Does not this repay us for all past troubles?'

For answer he stoops and kisses her on the lips.

THE END.

BILLING AND SONS, PRINTERS, GUILDFORD.